THE ELIXIR OF DENIAL

BOOKS BY CLARK

THE STAINS OF TIME

The Piano of Death

The Boot of Destiny

The Chains of Desire

The Elixir of Denial

The Dance of Dreams

OTHER BOOKS

Those Little Bastards

All He Left Behind

Missing Mr. Wingfield

The Seven Wives of Silver

Bad Poetry Night

Out of the Woods

Under the World

THE ELIXIR OF DENIAL

E. CHRISTOPHER CLARK

Published in the United States by Clarkwoods in Chelmsford, Massachusetts.

ISBN for the Print Edition: 978-1-952044-29-8
ISBN for the Digital Edition: 978-1-952044-28-1

Library of Congress Control Number: 2021921059

For Dana, who gave me my first dance in August 1996. With her quick wit and easy-going demeanor, she taught a nervous 18-year-old that strippers are people too. And all sex workers, for that matter.

I

IF I COULD TURN
BACK TIME

FALL 2007

❦ I ❦

A shley had spent a year trying to fuck the memory of Robin Gates out of her system, but it hadn't worked. Not at all. Because here she was again, with another stranger's head between her thighs—the twentieth, at least—and *still* she felt haunted. Because once the face was gone from view, once it was only the hair atop the stranger's head that Ashley could see, the stranger might as well have been Robin anyway. Robin had dyed her hair so many times, had cut it so many different ways, that Ashley's imagination had no trouble in running wild.

Afterward, smoking a cigarette on the balcony while the stranger dressed and collected their tip, Ashley tried again to count the number of bridges that spanned the rushing waters of the Willamette. A search on her phone could've told her, but she'd always been fond of doing things the hard way. The *honest* way. And besides: she'd left the phone back on the nightstand.

"Aren't you worried it'll be stolen?" That's what Robin would have said in a moment like this, what Ashley could hear the ghost of Robin saying right now.

"Do you worry that I'll steal your stuff when you fall asleep next to me?" That's what Ashley would have said in return.

Robin would've frowned at that. Then she would've said this was different. Ashley was her girlfriend, first of all. And second of all, Ashley was a stripper and not a prostitute.

On the balcony, Ashley sighed. She'd loved Robin, but the girl was not without her faults. Nor, it seemed, was her ghost.

There was a knock at the balcony's door. Ashley glanced over her shoulder to see what it was the stranger wanted. The tip had been sizable and the goodbye clear, or so Ashley had thought.

"You're not afraid someone will see you?" asked the stranger.

"Smoking?" said Ashley, with a coy grin.

"Naked," said the stranger, clarifying.

Ashley smiled as she took another drag. "Let them see," she said. "Let them see."

❧

THE NEXT DAY, before her red-eye home to Boston, Ashley took a walk through Old Town toward the Steel Bridge. Leaving the last of her cash in a series of outstretched hands along the way, and her suitcase of clothes at a nearby shelter, she made it to the middle of the sturdy old structure with naught but a bag of ashes to her name.

And a phone and a passport, she remembered. With a frown, she chided herself for being melodramatic.

As cars rumbled across the deck of the bridge above her, as cyclists whipped by behind her on the lower deck's walkway—even as a whistle in the distance signaled the imminent arrival of some lumbering train or another—Ashley stood still and silent. But thoughts raced across her mind as fast as the traffic speeding by all around her. And after a few minutes of trying and failing to slow them down, Ashley gave up. She grunted, frustrated with herself—frustrated by her inability to honor her lover's memory with even a *moment* of silence—and she unzipped the plastic bag. Then she reached in for a pinch of Robin's remains, so that she could get this over with.

"A pinch for every place I ever played." That had been Robin's request. And she'd played Portland twice: once at the Aladdin and once at the Roseland. So here Ashley was, to do the bidding of the deceased once again.

It occurred to Ashley then, as she reached into the bag for a second pinch, that maybe the reason she couldn't free herself from Robin's ghost was that she carried these pieces of Robin with her everywhere she went. And maybe if she just emptied everything out here, it would be over. And how would Robin even know? She was dead, after all.

Ashley listened for the voice of Robin's ghost on the breeze, waited for the wind to whisper *"I would know"* into her ear. But the wind said nothing. Robin, if she were out there somewhere, in some way—she said nothing. Maybe she *wanted* Ashley to let her go.

So Ashley unzipped the bag all the way this time and tipped the open maw toward the river below. She watched the last remains of her lost love slip ever closer to the precipice, reminding her of the sand in an hourglass. It would all be gone eventually, wouldn't it? All of it gone to the other side. So why not be done with it now?

But Ashley couldn't do it. She sealed the bag right back up and returned it to the safety of her sweatshirt's front pouch. If Ashley had done it, Robin might not have known. She *was* dead, true. But *Ashley* would have known. She would've had to live with knowing.

And she was *sick* of what she knew.

Back home in Boston, on the way from the airport to her family's house on Cape Cod, Ashley asked her cousin Matt if she could smoke in his car.

"Smoke?" asked Matt, confused.

"Smoke," said Ashley, shaking the cigarette at him in case he'd suddenly lost the ability to comprehend English.

"*That's* what you bought with the money you bummed off me?" he asked, grimacing as he spoke.

"Yeah," said Ashley. Then she pointed at the soda she'd slipped into his cup holder. "And the Coke."

Matt returned his focus to the road. Ashley, taking Matt's silence to be a "no," slipped the cigarette back into the pack. Then she rolled down the window and tossed the pack right out the side. The lighter, too.

Still, Matt said nothing.

As Ashley cranked on the handle to close the window again, she asked Matt if he knew there were buttons for this shit now.

"Never trusted those things," he said. "Besides, I like to do things the hard way."

He glanced at Ashley to see if she remembered their grandfather's old saying too.

"The honest way," she said, finishing the sentence.

So that was it, she realized. Matt was thinking about Grampy. Dead over ten years now and still haunting him—haunting Matt the way Robin was haunting Ashley. And why not? Matt had been there at Grampy's end, just as Ashley had been there at Robin's. Matt had been the *only* one there, actually—the only member of the family at Gramp's side in those last years, the years he spent hacking his lungs apart with cough after cacophonous cough.

The family had fractured over the matter of Matt's disastrous coming out, of course, and Grampy had taken the poor boy in. And so, Matt had been the one to buy Gramp his cigarettes when the old man was too weak to drive to the center of town to get them himself. Matt had been the one to drive Grampy to the hospital, to see the doctors he would hear but not heed. *Matt* had been the one to find his grandfather turning blue that April morning, slumped over the white porcelain of the toilet into which he'd coughed up a pool of his red, red blood—a tableau as All-American as it was tragic. Yep. That was all Matt. And he wasn't going to be a party to that kind of departure again.

"You have to special order these?" asked Ashley, pointing at the window crank and trying to change the subject.

Matt nodded.

"Whatcha gonna do when they don't even offer them on special orders anymore?"

Matt shrugged.

Ashley closed her eyes and sighed a heavy sigh. There was no getting away from this. He wanted answers. As much as he might hate them, he wanted them.

"I started years ago," she told him. "For work."

Though he kept his eyes on the road, he raised his right eyebrow—a signal for her to explain, to go on.

"I'd noticed a direct correlation between girls who smoked and girls who didn't," she said. "And though there was less of an impact on tips at the rail—"

"The rail?" he said.

"The rail along the stage," Ashley explained. "Anyway, the difference in tips collected on stage by smokers vs. non-smokers was statistically insignificant."

"But" said Matt, his voice pitching upward at the end of the word.

"*But* the difference between smokers and non-smokers when it came to private dances was impossible to ignore," said Ashley. "Not only did the smokers get dances more often, they were also more likely to get a second song out of a guy. *And* they pocketed significantly higher tips to boot."

"Do strippers have pockets?" asked Matt.

Ashley slugged him in the arm for the joke, but she felt

comforted that the amateur comedian inside her cousin was making an appearance at last. That meant she still had at least a *slight* chance at forgiveness.

"It's a phallic thing then?" asked Matt. "The cigarettes?"

Ashley nodded. "The customers just loved seeing something between a lady's lips. And if couldn't be their dicks, better that it be something so small it couldn't be seen as competition."

"You never tried a cigar?" asked Matt.

Ashley nodded. "Oh, I did," she said. "But there were only a few guys that seemed to work on. And they were generous, sure. But they were few and far between. I went back to cigs and made up the difference in volume in no time flat."

Matt shook his head at her, a smirk playing at his lips. "You are too smart to be taking off your clothes for a living," he said.

Ashley punched him again.

"I know, I know," said Matt, rubbing at his arm. "Female empowerment and all that. Reclaiming female desire and what-not. Which wave of feminism are we on now?"

Ashley knew he was joking, but she told him she was going to hit him again anyway if he didn't cut the shit.

"What I want to know," said Matt, as flicked on his blinker to signal his turn off one highway and onto the next, "is how you hid it from us all of these years."

"Nicorette when I'm around the family," she began.

"*That's* what you're always chewing?" he said, interrupting. "I thought it was Doublemint. Maybe Hubba Bubba."

"Altoids, hand lotion, and perfume," she continued, "same as I used at the club to keep the non-smokers from getting turned off by the reek of me."

"What about your teeth?" said Matt, glancing over at her quickly before returning his gaze to the road. "Gramp's teeth were yellow as all get-out near the end."

"I brush like a motherfucker," she said. "And I've made whitening strips my best friend."

They drove on in silence for a while, all of Matt's questions seemingly answered. But then, as they crossed over the Cape Cod Canal by way of the Sagamore Bridge, Matt piped up again.

"Aren't you scared?" he asked. "Knowing how Gramp died, aren't you the least bit—?"

"I see an oncologist once a month," she blurted out.

"Isn't that a lot?" asked Matt.

Ashley laughed. "Sure," she said, "but the doctor's *hot*."

THE SUN WAS RISING over Nantucket Sound as they pulled into the driveway, painting the sky above Red River Beach in shades of bronze and gold. Out on the lawn, Ashley's brother Michael was painting too—albeit on a slightly smaller canvas. And he was doing it wearing nothing but a pair of plaid boxer shorts and a sleeve of dried paint on each of his arms.

"What's he working on?" Ashley asked Matt.

Matt put the car in park and nodded toward the family's old barn, the walk-out basement of which had been converted into a small theater in recent years.

As they got out of the car, Ashley asked if the painting was for the website or a poster or something.

"Or something," said Matt, smirking and shaking his head. "Veronica and Desiree keep telling him he's taking too much time on it, that it was perfect the first three times, but he's been out here every morning this week. Showed up to Tracy's birthday party on Sunday with paint in his beard. And here he is, on his own birthday, sweating details no one will ever see—not when the damn thing is shrunk down to fit in the nav-bar of a website nobody's ever gonna visit, or in the corner of a poster that's just going to get covered up with a hundred other flyers down at the coffee shop."

"Business isn't as booming as Vern and Des hoped it would be?" asked Ashley.

"Well," said Matt, "when you're hoping a certain rock star will put you on the map by playing the closing show of her tour at your new venue, and then that closing show never happens..." He trailed off. "Sorry," he said, "I didn't mean to imply that Robin... that she... I mean, I know she didn't get shot on purpose."

Ashley gave him a gentle squeeze in the same place she'd punched him before, hoping he'd get the message that it was okay (since she didn't have the strength to say that out loud to someone yet again). A lot of shit had gone south since Robin was killed, more than Robin would ever know.

Unless she DOES know, Ashley thought to herself. Then she paused, listening again for the wind—for one particular voice floating upon it—but the air was still. Maddeningly still.

"I've been working on some plays about the family's history," said Matt with a sigh. "Seeing as everyone loves a story about a fall from grace," he said, "and our family's full of those."

They crept gingerly toward the front porch, careful not to disrupt the master at work on the front lawn—lest he soil his shorts in fright. And as they did, Ashley asked Matt what parts of the family's history he was working on.

"Well, I've got the coming out movie y'all are going to watch tonight," he began, nodding at Michael as he said "at the birthday boy's special request. Then," he said, "I've got this series about our great-grandfather's seven wives. You remember them, right?"

Ashley *did* remember them, one in particular.

"You doing one on the witch?" Ashley asked. "You doing one on Ada?"

Matt nodded. "I hope so. Toughest nut to crack, though. How to tell that story while still sounding plausible, given the things that woman believed and put down in her journal, given the yarns Grampy used to spin about her and her untimely demise."

Ashley didn't know why she hadn't told Matt—or anyone else

for that matter—that Grampy's crazy stories about Ada barely scratched the surface. But she hadn't. Maybe she thought they wouldn't believe her. Maybe she thought they'd chalk it all up to post-traumatic stress over being there when Robin was shot. But Ashley had seen Ada across the street the night of the murder, had seen with her own two eyes a woman who was supposed to have been killed 114 years beforehand. And before all that, Ashley had listened to Robin's stories about her encounters with Ada, about the obituary Robin found when she was a kid and how it spelled out her destiny. Ashley had seen and heard all manner of unbelievable things about Ada by this point, and she wasn't ready to be told she was crazy. Because she wasn't crazy.

Unless she was.

A chuckle from Matt brought her back to reality, and she asked him what was so funny.

"Have I ever told you," Matt began, "about the time we tried one of old Ada's potions out on Veronica?"

"No," said Ashley, trying to keep her jaw from falling to the floor. "I don't think you have."

Sitting in the theater that night, surrounded by family and friends buzzing about what her cousin's film would show—and how far it would go—Ashley stewed. She stewed in her seat like it was a pot and she was the meat. And maybe the potatoes, too. She stewed in a broth of newfound knowledge, and she felt herself boiling from the inside out.

Is that even how boiling works? she wondered to herself.

Ashley felt a tug on her sleeve and turned to face her mother. "Are you alright?" Mum whispered.

Ashley nodded and smiled. "Just nervous is all. You know how Matt likes to push the envelope."

Mum nodded now. Smiled, too. She gave Ashley's arm a squeeze, then returned her attention to the slideshow playing on screen—a collection of old family photos fading in and out as a sort of prelude to the main attraction.

Ashley did her best now to keep from boiling over, did her best to keep her stewing to a simmer. But she couldn't stop thinking about what Matt had told her that morning. He had drugged Veronica with a potion stolen from one of Ada's old journals. It had all turned out for the best, Matt told Ashley, certain that she was blanching because of the way Veronica had been violated. "Look at it this way," Matt explained. Vern had finally left her dumb-ass husband, she'd run into the arms of the woman she'd loved since they were kids, and now they were living happily ever after.

But it wasn't Veronica that Ashley was thinking about. It wasn't what they'd done to Veronica that had Ashley turning white as a ghost. It was the potion, and what it could do.

Because, if the potion could let Veronica revisit her past, then why wouldn't it work for Ashley too? And how hard could it be to bring back a souvenir? Even if that souvenir were a person, something flesh and blood instead of a plush toy or mug shaped like a cartoon duck's head—how hard could it be? Really?

Ashley closed her eyes and imagined herself pulling a smiling Robin out of the shadows and back into the light, and the thought made her smile too.

Then a crack of thunder rattled the theater, so loud through the speakers that surrounded her on all sides that Ashley imagined Zeus and Thor hurling bolts at each other to prove—once and *for all*—whether it was the Greeks or the Norsemen who had the bigger dicks.

Ashley opened her eyes just in time to see the movie screen fade in from black.

Her grandfather's cottage stood defiant against the winds whipping off of Nantucket Sound. Freshly painted blue shutters slapped against the weathered gray-brown shingles of the place, but the house itself shrugged off the bitter breath of their family's cranky, middle-aged God.

For more than three-hundred years, the descendants of Silas Silver had lived here. And for every house that had fallen—and every Silas—another had risen in its place. Even after the memorable gale of 1844, which had taken half of the house and all but the boot of their patriarch, the Silvers had just kept on keeping on.

Ashley's grandfather stood on the front porch now, and she marveled at the sight of him. Only here, on the big screen, could he stand as tall as she'd always imagined him to be. Ash watched as that lovely old man, now thirty feet tall, stooped over to liven her mother's lemonade. He emptied a bottle of Stoli into the glass pitcher, gave it a swirl, then took a sip. Then he smacked his lips together, licked them just as smidge, and nodded.

"Just the ticket," he said. Then he looked back over his shoulder to check on something.

The film cut then to a close-up of a window, a birthday cake cooling on the sill. Ashley had known *where* he was right from the start. Now, at last, she knew *when*. Though of course it shouldn't have been much of a surprise. Matt, whether making a film or telling a story around a campfire, had never been one to beat around the bush. He'd cut right to the chase, right to the day in question. That was just how he rolled.

Up on the big screen, it was August 31, 1989—Ashley's 10th birthday. The day of their family's great schism. Mum was behind the camcorder, Ashley realized now. She'd gotten it earlier that month, when she turned 32—just three years older than Ashley was now. Ash tried to remember if Mum ever turned the camera on herself that day. There were plenty of pictures of her from back then, but it'd be a hoot to see her up on the big screen—late-eighties hair and all.

But it was Grampy back on screen again, not Mum. He was still sipping at the lemonade, and still smiling, but now Ashley could see a weariness in his eyes. And she watched him catch himself and try to shake the look off his face and out of his body. *Weariness*. When had he gotten old enough to be *weary*?

Ashley imagined him thinking about his father as he sighed, his old man. Because that's what Grampy was now: the old man. The oldest of men, it felt like. He could only pray that if he lived as long as his father—another 25 years—he would never become as shriveled and bitter. He'd rather die.

And he was going to.

Ashley knew that all too well. The old man on the movie screen had only five years left. Not even. Ash started to count off on her fingertips. No, it wasn't five years at all. He'd be gone in four and change.

But for now he was still there. He was still *here*.

Grampy watched the giggling children of summer renters run from the sands of Red River Beach as the storm rolled in, watched them as they raced down Old Wharf Road with their towels held over their heads. The torrent bombarded the weakening walls of the sand castles they'd left behind. Steam rose off of the hot black pavement. And Ashley could see in her grandfather's face a longing to be on the road again, with his trumpet and his best girl and all of the old gang. As he smiled, she felt him longing for the swelter of a New Orleans dive in the middle of July—his sweat so heavy and thick that the music felt like real work for once.

The film cut to the birthday cake again. Then back to the shot of Grampy as his nose caught the scent, as he wiggled his nostrils for the camera. An old favorite of the kids and the grandkids, that gesture. But he pretended like no one was watching. He was no actor, had no training to speak of, but he knew enough not to break the fourth wall.

"Tomorrow begins the fall," he said to no one in particular. And no one in particular corrected him. No one would dream of correcting him, of letting him know that tomorrow was only September the first. No one was going to tell Grampy Silver that summer didn't end for another twenty some-odd days. He knew what he was talking about, thank you very much. At least when it came to things like the seasons, goddamn it.

He sipped some more lemonade. "Has it really been so long," he said, "since I unlocked these windows and threw open those shutters? Wasn't it just yesterday that I took my sister's old easel out the attic and set it up for Michael? And how long can it have been since Trevor hiked over from Hyannis to tune the piano for Veronica? A whole summer?" He shook his head. "For Christ's sake," he said, waving his free hand toward the barn he'd made a garage the moment this land was his and his alone. "Matthew and I still haven't gotten that goddamned jalopy started."

The camera held on an over-the-shoulder shot of Gramps as he walked toward the porch swing. The barn was in the background, obscured by sheets of rain, but Ashley was feeling more confident than ever of where Matt was going to take the film next. And she wasn't sure she wanted to be sitting next to Mum when it happened.

Grampy leaned across the porch swing and poked his head out into the rain.

The old man stood there like that for a long while—eyes closed, smiling as raindrops pelt his buzz-cut head. Ashley had the same bad skin that he did, so she knew how much this must've stung at first. But she also knew how relieving it would eventually be, to feel the rain soothing the patches of scalp he'd scratched raw during his morning argument with the eczema that'd plagued him since boyhood.

His eyes blinked open, and he stared intently off screen. Stared, Ashley realized with a knowing nod, at the barn.

She cast a quick glance at her mother in the seat next to her, just to see what Mum was thinking. But that woman was as much a blank slate as she always was, just staring intently at the screen. Inscrutable. Unreadable.

Grampy shouted over the deluge, and brought Ashley's attention back to the film. "I wish I could do more for *her*," he said. "At least today. It is her birthday, after all."

The film held on his melancholy face just long enough to show that he meant it, then cut to as unsteady a handheld shot as Ashley had ever seen on a big screen. It was Mum walking across the yard, Ash imagined. Mum was in the rain, holding the camera in place on one shoulder while she tried to keep the whole kit and caboodle dry under the umbrella she clutched in her free hand. And Ashley could remember that umbrella, all of a sudden: a black beast of a thing she hadn't thought about in years, with Michael Keaton's Batman emblazoned upon it. One of her birthday presents that year. Or, well, it was *supposed* to be. But then the storm had come, and there were no others to be found, and her mother was never one for sentiment when practicality was also a concern. So she'd torn the wrapping paper off of it, unfurled it, and put it to good use.

Ashley remembered Mum shaking it out as she stepped into the garage and found her—as the camera found her now—staring at the pin-up calendar that hung in there, in that place where girls weren't meant to be.

The garage was dark and cool in the summers of her youth—a refuge from the heat, from her family, and from the boys who stared too long at her on the beach. A refuge too from the dirty old men, those fucking *dinosaurs*, who not only stared too long but stared too *hard* to boot. Who stared *at all*. Did they not realize she was 10?

She. Was. *10*.

So Ashley liked to sit in the garage by herself, in quiet solitude, in the rumble seat of the old Ford, and she liked to brainstorm what she'd say to those perve-balls once she worked up the guts to say anything at all.

But mostly, as the film emphasized right that second, Ashley liked to look at the calendar. She liked to imagine that one day she'd learn how to use the power she had, just like the girls on calendars and magazines did. She was just a New Mutant now, but she dared to dream that someday she'd be an X-Man

But if Ashley had a mentor, someone to teach her that with great beauty came great responsibility, it was her mother. And Ashley felt about her mum the way Kitty Pryde felt about Professor Charles Xavier in *Uncanny X-Men* #168. Only Ash wasn't about to turn around right now and shout "Doctor Silver is a jerk!" because, well, even though she'd get away with it by giving Mum puppy dog eyes afterward, she knew that Mum was right: with great beauty came great responsibility.

But how could she not know that was a Spider-Man quote she was riffing on, and not from the X-Men?! Like *how?!*

Mum set the camera down on the bumper of the car, just enough of the chrome in the shot that Ashley got a total 80s flashback when she noticed the reflection of the big, honking contraption. But the story on screen pulled her right back in, her mother stepping into frame.

"You still you think it's weird?" asked Mum

Ashley remembered how close she stood, Mum's shoulder brushing against her own. She felt like Mum wanted to hug her or something. But she didn't want to be hugged. In fact, she wanted to take a step away from her. But she didn't, because she knew that Mum would just close the distance anyway.

"It's weird," said Mum.

"What?" said Ashley. And though she knew this wasn't what Mum meant by *weird*, she added: "That Grampy keeps a calendar that's 15 years old?"

Mum fingered the pages of the calendar, flipped forward to September, then October, and so on. Then she let it fall back to August.

In the theater watching this, Ashley laughed at a detail she had never noticed: her grandfather's calendar might have been 15 years out of date, but he still kept it on the correct month.

"She was a beautiful woman," Mum mused.

"She still is," said Ashley. "Only she's not *Grampy's* woman."

Mum turned, the camera catching her in profile as she set a hand on her daughter's shoulder. "She was never *anyone's* woman," Mum told Ashley.

Ash studied her mother's face—both the Ash on screen and the one in the movie theater right now—trying to find some emotion there (since her steady, trained doctor's voice gave nothing away). But Ashley didn't find anything in Mum's eyes then, and she couldn't see them clearly enough now.

The ten-year-old Ashley on the screen shrugged off her mother's hand. She shook a finger at Mum, then at the calendar, as she asked, "Why *does* my father's father have a pin-up calendar of my mother's mother anyway?"

"Ashley," said Mum, laughing a little as she shook her head. "Every garage on the east coast had this calendar on their walls. My dad gave them away with every spare part he sold. A catalog and a calendar of photos he shot of his wife. It's how they built their business."

"But why did Grampy keep it?" asked Little Ashley, and Older Ashley noted that she—*Me*, Ashley reminded herself—didn't seem to give two shits about Grampy appreciating the beauty of another woman. What concerned her—*Me*, thought Ashley again —was who this particular woman was.

Mum put a hand on each of Little Ashley's shoulders now. "His wife's been gone seven years now, Ash. And *her* husband"— Mum nodded at the calendar—"has been gone twice as long. They're close, Ash. They always have been."

Little Ashley squinted and grimaced. Through clenched teeth, she mumbled a mumble so garbled by the camera that Matt had inserted a subtitle: "How close?"

Silence. Mum didn't answer. And Matt let it hang there, let the viewer imagine the unsaid.

Good on you, thought Ashley, because this was the moment that Matt's film good and truly won her over. She was proud that he, unlike so many in their family—unlike *himself*, most of the time— had learned to appreciate the power of subtlety and nuance. Ambiguity, too.

Up on the screen, Little Ashley turned her attention back to the calendar. Then the film cut to a panning close-up of the calendar, obviously filmed years afterward. And Ashley marveled once again at the beauty of her mother's mother. In one photo, she was seated on the hood of a rusted jalopy, the polish of her every aspect standing in stark contrast. She wore a crocheted body suit with a plunging neckline, intricate patterns of white yarn pulled tight over tanned flesh. Beneath the bare minimum of fabric needed to keep her breasts from spilling out, the suit opened again to reveal her midriff. A pattern of diamond-shaped openings ran down her side, down over her hip, down the legs she'd crossed one over the other. It looked like her eyes were closed, but really they were focused on the hand that was pulling a lock of golden hair away from her perfect head. Every inch of her skin was a shade of bronze; there was make-up also, but nothing that drew attention away from the monochromatic mix of beiges and browns, coffees and chocolates.

The film cut back to Little Ashley and her mother then. Mum was *still* staring at the calendar, but Little Ashley wasn't. Not anymore. No, she was staring at Mum now instead. And something about the tableau struck the older Ashley sitting in the movie theater right now: what she was looking at just then wasn't *just* a mother and a daughter. It was *two* daughters, each of them marveling at the beauty of the woman who'd made them—each of them trying to puzzle it out. *How did she get so pretty?* they each wondered. *And how can I do the same?*

If only they would look at each other and say "You don't have to *do* anything."

If only they could look at themselves and say that.

"It's all an exercise in titillation anyway," said Mum. "See the way the stiletto's dangling from her naked foot? See the way that cloth is juxtaposed against flesh."

The juxtaposition of cloth and flesh, Ashley thought to herself as she shook her head. That was title of her brother's goddamned dissertation, right there in the aphorism of her mother. *When had she said that to Michael?* she wondered. And then: *did he give credit to Mum in the book?* She wasn't sure, because she still hadn't read it.

Little Ashley pulled a bag of potato chips from the pixelated shadows of the past, and she pulled her older counterpart back into the film as she did so. Then she plunged a greasy hand into the depths of the bag. Older Ashley smiled as she remembered fishing around for those last few crumbs.

And now, of course, she had a craving for Lay's Sour Cream and Onion—because *of course she did*. Only there was no hope of calming that craving, because they didn't carry Sour Cream and Onion at the concession stand. Which was *sacrilege*. Her cousins said they were trying to keep the odor in the space to a minimum, but fuck that. Hadn't they ever heard of theater of the *nose*?

"...the right piece of fabric in the right place," said the Mum on screen. "That's all it is."

And she was right. Varicose veins crept like vines along the length of Mum's hips and thighs, but no one would ever know that. And no one would ever care. Because Mum knew, like her mother before her, how to use the cut of her jeans to her advantage. Or the color of her stockings when she went to work. Or the flowing Palazzo pants she wore over her bikini bottoms at the beach—so that she looked like a model walking a runway when she sauntered from shoreline to sand castle to hand her children pails of water for their moat. Ashley remembered well the way those pants clung to her bottom, even though they flowed and flared out everywhere else.

She was a master, Ashley's mother. Ash saw how the men at her father's company picnics looked at her—hating to see her leave, but loving to watch her go. And Ashley wasn't deaf either. She heard her brother's friends teasing him during their sleepovers, making crude jokes and bold proclamations.

"And," said Mum, wrapping an arm around Little Ashley's shoulder and giving her the hug she'd been waiting to give from the start. "Nobody knew that better than Grammy Silver. She was... what is the word Grampy likes to use?"

"Substantial," said Little Ashley.

"Yes," said Mum. "Edna—Grammy Silver—was a *substantial*

woman. And she was a *dish*. Being big didn't make her any less beautiful."

"But it did make her die," said Little Ashley. Then she shrugged off her mother's arm, stood, and stomped away.

"It did not," said Mum. "And you know that. It was her brain that betrayed her, not her body."

Little Ashley—or just plain *Ashley* now, for maybe the first time—ran her hand along the Ford's front bumper, heading toward the camera but not looking at it. She peered down at her reflection in the chrome, and it made her want to cry. She searched and searched for some trace of Grammy Silver in the girl staring back at her. But she couldn't find anything. All she saw was her mother, and her mother before her. And that felt like a betrayal somehow, like she'd *decided* which of them she was going to look like and she'd picked the ones who everyone agreed were beautiful. The ones who never had to work for it. The ones who never had to work for *anything*.

"Why would you say that?" asked Mum. "Why would you say that, Ash?"

Why *would* she say it? Why would she spurn the woman who made her blueberry muffins every morning of every summer, even when Mum tried to convince her that it was okay to just pour the kids a bowl of cereal every once in a while? Why would she spurn the woman who had done that for her, even in that last summer, when she could barely remember how to turn on the stove?

Grammy Silver taught Ashley how to open the light blue top of the Jiffy box without dusting the countertop in a poof of its pre-mixed ingredients. She showed her how to pour it into the flour bowl, the bowl Ash and her mother had painted with flowers that last year to help Grammy out. And even when there was almost nothing left of her inside that brain and that body that were conspiring against her, she could still put on a clinic about how to crack an egg. Not even a shred of shell fell into her mixing bowls. No, ma'am. And even when she forgot Ashley's name—even when she was little more than a husk herself, she could still get the split husk of an egg into the open maw of the now-empty Jiffy box without a drop of yolk hitting her kitchen table.

Grammy Silver was a miracle—an orphan of immigrant parents who'd been broken by the broken dream of their new broken country, a kid who'd survived the explosion of a still in the basement of the bootleggers who fostered her, a woman who'd pieced together a broken man and made a husband of him. She was a *miracle*, as brilliant a light in this dim universe as ever there was.

And yet: she was fat. And Ashley didn't want to be fat. She didn't want to be cast aside by her friends and banished from the playground to the back field. She didn't want to hang with the Cabbage Patch kids at recess, those oddly shaped oddballs in their frumpy Care Bears sweats, with nothing to talk about but which Wuzzle they wanted for Christmas. So she'd abandoned her. After Grammy died, Ashley had *abandoned* her.

And Grammy had loved Ashley the most. She *had!* She had loved Ashley the most of all her grandchildren, because she'd only had sons herself, she'd always wanted a girl, and her first grand-daughter—Veronica—could never be bothered to dally with dolls. Or with being dolled up.

She'd loved Ashley most, but Ashley had cast her Grammy Silver out of her body like some witch casting some spell. And it didn't matter that Ashley wanted her back now, now that she'd realized what she'd done. It was too late.

On screen, the younger Ashley fought the urge to punch the car. She fought the *overwhelming* desire to knock the block off the pretty little bitch staring back at her. How *dare* she cry right now? She didn't have the right. She had no idea. *None.*

"You think I'm lying to you?" said Mum.

"No," said Ashley. "You're telling me what the beautiful people always tell the ugly people."

"Ashley," Mum began, and she might've laughed if she hadn't sighed first. "You are not ugly."

Ashley faced her mother. "No, Mum," she said. "I am. On the inside, I'm the ugliest person you've ever met."

"Ashley," she said, "that's not—"

"It *is*," said Ashley. And then she stalked away from her mother. She threw open the side door and stomped out into the rain.

Within seconds, she was drenched. And the makeup she'd put on that morning while she was playing dress up—it all began to run. And that made Ashley smile. For the first time that day, she smiled. Because she imagined the rain washing away every pretty part of herself, so that all that was left was the rotten. The ugly.

But maybe—just *maybe*—if she stood out there long enough, the rain would wash that away too. And maybe, buried somewhere beneath all of that ugliness, was the woman she was looking for.

It's there, Ashley wanted to tell her younger self. *But you're never going to find it alone.*

In the theater, as the film cut to a title card meant to introduce the next part, Mum squeezed Ashley's hand. And while it wasn't the hand she wished she was holding right that second, Ashley squeezed back. For now, the uncomplicated embrace of her mother would have to do.

But tonight, when this was all over, she was going to get a vial of Ada's potion out of her cousin. And then she was going to find the woman who'd helped her find herself. And she was going to bring her back to life.

᪥   3   ᪥

When Ashley asked Matt where he kept the potion, he told her that he didn't have any, that "the kid is the keeper."

He shook his chin in the direction of his niece, who was stacking the audience's chairs with her two best friends, the three of them laughing the shrill but boisterous laughter of teenage girls.

"Tracy?" asked Ashley. And when Matt nodded, when he nodded while smiling that sly smirk of his, Ashley's jaw fell. "But she's only 14," she said.

"She's a good kid," said Matt, waving goodbye to a gray-haired couple on their way out of the theater. "She keeps me honest," he said, "knows to ask the tough questions before she hands it over"

"How do you know she's not using it herself?" asked Ashley.

Matt's goofy grin disappeared. He looked deadly serious as he repeated "She's a good kid."

And so it was that Ashley found herself knocking on Tracy's door that evening. Knocking, then waiting. Waiting, and wondering what questions Tracy would ask *her*.

The door creaked open just a smidge at first, but Tracy threw it open with gusto as soon as she realized who it was. "Auntie!" she said, wrapping her arms around Ashley, then pulling her inside.

"The girls took the bed," said Tracy, shaking a nonchalant thumb at the two friends from earlier, who were cuddled together on Tracy's bed now and seemingly fast asleep. "My chair is super-comfy, though," she continued, gesturing for Ashley to take the seat.

"Where'll you sit?" Ashley began to ask, but before she could finish Tracy had already copped a squat on the sleeping bag strewn across her floor.

"Are you here about the potion?" asked Tracy, getting right to the point.

Ashley grinned. God, how she loved this kid. Tracy was the best of all of them: as deferential and caring as Veronica, as obsessed with details as Michael, as smart and full of mischief as Matt, and as straight and to the point as Ashley herself.

"You want to see Robin again," said Tracy, "right?"

Ashley nodded.

"Why?"

There were a million reasons, weren't there? That's what Ashley found herself thinking in that moment. But these reasons were like the keys with wings in Harry Potter: just out of reach. And Ashley didn't have a broomstick to ride on so that she could catch one. So when Tracy repeated her question, all Ashley could think to say was "Because she was the love of my life."

Tracy raised an eyebrow, an eyebrow that might as well have been a question mark. And the question she was asking—without even having to ask it aloud—was a fair one: could there ever truly be just *one* love of Ashley Silver's life? One love to rule them all and whatnot?

No. Because before Robin, it had been David. Before David, it had been Adam. And during her time with Robin, hadn't she also loved Ryan? And who was to say that she wouldn't ever love again? Robin wouldn't have. If she had lived, she'd have stuck with

Ashley to the end. Robin, for all her polyamorous tendencies, was a monogamist at heart. But Ashley?

"Auntie?" said Tracy, a hint of tenderness in her voice—because even if she was tasked with asking the tough questions, she could still empathize with those she interrogated.

"She's a song," said Ashley, not quite sure where the words were coming from. "She's a song I can't get out of my head."

Tracy nodded. "And you need to hear it one more time," she said. "All the way through, or else you'll never escape it."

A tear rolled down Ashley's cheek, then another. It felt like a betrayal to nod, to confirm that everything she'd just said was true, but nod she did.

Tracy nodded now too, then leaned toward what Ashley had taken to be nothing more than a nightstand. She pushed aside a tablecloth to reveal the door to a mini-fridge, opened it, then reached inside.

What she pulled from the refrigerator and handed to Ashley were two small vials of clear liquid. And she handed them over gingerly, with great care. These were the last two vials she had for now. There was a new batch brewing, but it wouldn't be done for a month.

"The first time," said Tracy, "take it straight up. Get used to the feeling. See where your heart takes you. Learn how to navigate the trip."

Ashley nodded.

"The second time," she said, "you add a bit of Robin to the mix. You've still got some of her ashes left, right?"

Ashley nodded again.

Tracy stood and gestured toward the door. "Best to take it right before bed. It's safer when you're asleep."

Ashley stood and looked Tracy in the eye, which she realized involved looking up now. She wanted to ask how Tracy knew to take it before bed, if it was from personal experience. She felt like she was obligated, as the adult in the situation, to make sure her niece was being safe, but she also wanted to get to business. And even though Tracy *was* a good kid, she was still a kid. A teenager. And who knew if she'd chafe at being questioned so and take back the gift she'd just given?

Tracy hugged Ashley again, then bid her goodnight.

❦

BACK IN HER ROOM, Ashley sat on the edge of her bed and contemplated the two vials on her nightstand. And the bag of Robin's ashes, which sat beside them. And the door, which she could walk through right now if she wanted to—which she could walk through right now and never see again.

If she wanted to, which she didn't.

Did she?

She picked up one of the two vials and unscrewed its cap. Then she brought it to her lips. But before she drank it, she considered whether she should just get right to the point and mix in a bit of Robin's ashes right now. She appreciated Tracy's suggestion on how to handle this, to take baby steps, but she wasn't a baby and the kid's suggestion was just that: a *suggestion*.

But the kid was smart, smarter than Ashley had ever been. And maybe she should listen for once. She didn't want to screw things up when she went after Robin, right?

Ashley threw back her head and downed the potion in one gulp. Then she fell back into her nest of pillows and let the journey begin.

She followed where her heart led her. Her heart, and the ancient blood which pumped through it.

❦

THE NEXT THING SHE KNEW, she was no longer herself.

She was split open, the stuff of life spilling from her aching womb onto a bed of straw. Ashley looked down at the body that was no longer her own, and saw more blood. It was smeared across her belly and her chest, too. Her chest—where a child rested now, shivering.

No, not a child. A baby. A *newborn*.

He shivered less than she did, cradled as he was between her warm breasts, but still he reached out for something to steady himself. Her heartbeat, Ashley realized—that was what he was trying to hang onto. His tiny fist opened and closed around the air, grasping for the sound that was roaring in his ears, the sound that he felt as a quaking throughout the supple bones of a head that was not yet firmly on his shoulders. He would hold onto that sound with all his might, if only he could find it in the darkness.

Ashley saw him struggling. She saw him reaching out for that part of her that he could not have—that she could not give him even if she wanted to—and she offered up all that she did have instead, trying to get him to suckle as she murmured to her husband to find more blankets—her husband?!—to find them now, before the well-wishers came.

But the well-wishers were already here, he told her, or at least the first of them was: a gawking boy at the stable door who was mumbling something about voices on the wind compelling him to come, who was asking now if he should be play for them on his drum. His music, he told them, his voice quavering as he spoke, was the only gift he had to offer.

She nodded. *She*, this other woman Ashley had become, who Ashley realized now must be an ancestor of some sort—a relative. That's how the potion was supposed to work. But who was she?

The little drummer boy began to play, and something clicked in Ashley. And instead of hearing the song that he actually played, she heard in her head a Christmas song that wouldn't be written for centuries. And she wondered if this woman she'd become could really be she thought she was. And could the *baby* really be who she thought *he* was? Because Grampy had always said they were descended from Judas, not...

But now Ashley was thinking the thoughts of this woman, who was pondering the idea that her son might belong someday to someone other than her. It was an idea her own mother had taught her never truly takes hold, even after the child has grown and shared the bed of another. She was still not used to this idea, did not want to get used to it, but she knew what the voices had told her. She knew what was to come.

She *knew*, Ashley realized, and yet she pressed on. Because what else could she do?

❧

SUDDENLY, Ashley was herself again. But she was pretending to be someone else in the moment she'd traveled to. So often in her life, that was what had been called for. So often, that was what had worked.

It was a scene from the movie *Mallrats* that had inspired this particular look, the one where the girl showed off the code she used for keeping track of all the guys she'd slept with. A smiley face meant one thing, a smiley face with a wink meant another. And though Ashley hated that movie, she *loved* that look. And she knew the guys at school did, too.

So, just before school started that fall, she went shopping to assemble the outfit that Tricia Jones wore as she sat between the two guys who'd asked to see her journal. Dark-blue v-neck, white collared shirt, a pleated skirt of blue and green plaid—and the knee-high white socks, of course.

That outfit. *Oh*, that outfit and the much-wanted attention it had garnered after Ashley's breakup with Adam. And the action. The *action* it got her. The memory of David's head between her thighs, the skirt like a holy garment on the top of his bobbing pate.

Or like a kerchief, like the kerchief that her great-grand-mother wore in the only picture Ashley had ever seen of the poor woman. The poor woman who might've lived a life more like Ashley's, if only she'd been born a few decades later than she was.

❧

A MOTHER'S HELPER—THAT'S what her daughter told the grandchildren she was, ages and ages after she was gone. She'd crossed the Atlantic, indentured to some well-off family, and she took care of their children while they drank and cavorted and made headlines with every breath they took.

Like Ashley did now. Only Ashley wasn't Ashley anymore. She was Laima instead. Her great-grandmother.

And Laima—well, Laima only rated the front page once: on the day after she killed herself. "Twice widowed and despondent," they said of her, beneath the vulgar headline.

And that headline. That *fucking* headline. Ashley wanted to scream it out loud, to shout it in the face of the person who wrote it, but she couldn't scream anything now. Because she was Laima, not Ashley, and she was dying on the cold linoleum of her kitchen floor. No words would cross her lips again, those pink things that had begun to go blue, that would soon enough drain of all color altogether.

They could have put it bluntly and succinctly, by printing the word SUICIDE and leaving it at that, but that wouldn't have sold as many papers. Instead they shouted the details to the world—all in capital letters, mind you, so that nobody could miss them: FOUND DEAD WITH GAS TUBE IN MOUTH.

The story the paper told, it was the same one her daughter gave to the grandchildren some fifty years later. Grammy found her mother after coming inside for a drink of water, her skin flush from playing outside in the cold March air—from playing and *freezing* in the tattered coat and scarf that were all her mother could afford. She found Laima on the floor—near the oven, on her back, her body still warm—but she was too scared to call for help.

She tried to bring her mother back. Grammy tried to remember how hard her mother had pounded on her father's chest years before, on the day she'd tried to save him from his own tragic end. Grammy tried to remember how hard, and how many times—but it was no good. And Ashley, lying there helpless inside her great-grandmother's dying husk, wanted to reach out and hold her grandmother to her bosom, to tell her that she had done her best, that she loved her. But she couldn't, because that hadn't happened. And that's how this potion worked. You could see the past—you could *live* it—but you couldn't change it.

And so, the little girl version of Grammy Silver did what she did—what she had always done and would always do, because that's how history worked. She walked to the only relation she had left, an uncle two towns away. Melting snow soaked her socks through the cracks of her worn-out shoes. But she trudged on, leaving behind what was left of her mother.

What *was* left?

Though it hurt Ashley to think of her grandmother looking down at the graying skin of the corpse on the kitchen floor— though it made her heart ache—that is not where she felt betrayed.

She felt betrayed by what came next.

And what came next was the paper getting its digs in, the newspaper men informing their gentle, constant reader that Laima's home was "typical" of that area, with "no improvements" and "few furnishings." They gave her credit for her garden— credit, and perhaps a little grudging respect—but then they took even that away. They continued with a note that the city aided her from time to time, as if that was supposed to excuse something. As if their *aid* was a "get out of the shit house" card or something.

Just how much did they aid *you*, Ashley wondered. And how often? And how sincerely?

Laima had a hard time getting on, the paper said; her daughter was just *that much* more than she could bear. And all of this got Ashley to wondering where Laima's help was when she needed it. Where was *her* help—the woman who had once been a girl, the girl who had once been the mother's helper?

If only Laima could have had *herself*.

If only she hadn't lost herself somewhere along the way.

🕸

AND NOW ASHLEY had lost herself again. But she was herself, at least. And as the fog of memory lifted, it didn't take her long to realize where she was. But the dude standing across from her was still a mystery.

The two of them were standing under the awning of a Dunkin Donuts. Catching sight of her reflection in the store's window, Ashley realized she was dressed down for the day: sweats, a t-shirt, her hair in a ponytail. But even dressed down, she looked a cut above the schlub standing across from her. He was rocking a B's cap and an out of control beard, and he was sipping coffee from a paper cup that was steaming like it was the middle of February—only it could have also been a random day in June, because that was New England for you.

"I'm sorry," said Ashley, "you're going to need to jog my memory."

"In a car," he said, only it came out without the R. "On Route 6 down the Cape," he said. "In the dark," he added. (In the d*ah*k, dude.) Then he smirked and nodded, as if Ashley had given him some signal she'd finally remembered—which she was pretty sure she hadn't. "We was pulled over," he said, "and waiting for a statie to finish ticketing my buddy for failing to use his fucking blinker. And you—"

Ashley wanted to lose her shit right then and there at the way he said blink*ah*, but that wasn't what happened. Instead, she smiled at the memory which he'd succeeded in jogging: the memory of his fingers running through her hair near the end of it. She remembered how he'd warned her in a whisper, "Ash, baby, it's about to happen," and how he'd remembered her name. Even though she didn't remember his, even back then. She remembered how she'd told him it was okay, then how she'd swallowed out of guilt.

AND IT WAS GUILT which brought her from one place to the next this time. Guilt was the current which sped her along the river of dreams toward her next destination. Guilt, and a desire to rid people of it.

The goat rested on the girl's lap as she plucked briars from the back of his neck. He'd managed to rid himself of the rest with a frantic roll through the weeds, but these last few just wouldn't come loose. And so: he had gone to the place where the girl played. And he had leapt over another row of bushes to get there, chancing further aggravation in the hope she would set him free.

She was patient, this girl—Ashley's other grandmother—the only one her little brother would sit still for on Sunday mornings, when it was time to comb his angry mop of tangled blonde hair. She pulled the briars from the goat's fur with the same diligence, the same care. If there was a choice between yanking a hair and pricking her finger, she would bleed before hurting him.

Years from now, when she has crossed the ocean and made her way to America, when she has married the mechanic who will only make love to her after he has made love to the bottle, she will remember the goat in the weeds. She will remember to stroke the hair of the man who has done what is expected of him, even as he cries into the warmth of her bosom. She will work her fingers across his scalp inch by inch, rubbing and scratching, rubbing and scratching, until every hurt is gone, until he—like the goat—is staring into the middle distance.

Staring. Just *staring*. Unsure of how he got here, but thankful just the same.

Ashley had seen that look in a man's eyes many a time, but never in *this* man's eyes. Never before today. Because he died before she was born.

But now she had seen it, and there was a beauty there that broke her. A serenity that only a woman's touch could bring. And though she'd never felt guilty about the ways she'd used her body to make her way through life, she'd never been quite so proud as she was now. She'd never felt quite so aware of the possibilities, of the good that she might have done. That she might do still.

BUT OF COURSE, sometimes you don't have to be good to do good. Sometimes it helped to be bad instead. And so, the place she went next was the bathroom of an abandoned highway rest stop.

"The motel will be just as filthy," she told Robin. And though Robin had fucked too many dudes in that motel while on tour, and knew that the reputation which preceded it was built on foundations of hyperbole—though Robin *knew* that, she acquiesced to Ashley's request anyway.

Leaning against the wall while Robin went to town on her, Ashley stared at the dicks graffitied onto nearly every inch of the concrete that surrounded them. Her ass pressed against the cold metal of the handicap rail, the cave paintings of migrant neanderthals doing their best to distract her, it took Ashley *forever* to come.

When they switched, Robin affected a lisp and joked that she'd sprained her tongue in the effort.

Later, in the not-at-all filthy motel room—beneath a set of

freshly laundered sheets, in fact—Robin confessed that she had stared at the menagerie of members too, when it was her turn. And the two of them laughed themselves to sleep that night, debating which cartoonish prick they'd seen might actually be fun to fuck.

❧

IT WAS weird where the potion and the stream of consciousness took her next, but Ashley had long since abandoned any squeamishness about the fact that her parents used to fuck, or their parents before them. And so, she didn't so much as flinch when she found herself in the body of her grandfather now—the young man who would grow up to be Grampy.

It was midsummer, and he was rowing the girl worth wooing out onto Long Pond. The goal was teach her how to fish with a net, and she *did* smile at him as he cast it out onto the water. Later, when he was shivering beneath the blankets and telling his father the story of how he'd fell in, the old man told him that wasn't how wooing was done.

"She likes the idea of the fish being caught," said Grampy's father. "And the *idea* of the fisherman catching it, but just the idea. Never the real thing."

The next night, the girl worth wooing snuck in through Grampy's window. She'd come to check on him, to see if he was warm again. And he was, but not warm enough for her liking—not nearly warm enough. So she pressed her body against his and proved his father wrong.

That night, and a lifetime of nights thereafter. Because of course the girl worth wooing was Grammy, who'd pressed her warm body against the cold body of her own mother once upon a time—and she was never again going to fail the people she loved. Never again.

She couldn't change history, but history could change her.

AND OF COURSE, it was that thought which brought Ashley to her final destination: a sidewalk in Cambridge, Massachusetts, a few minutes past midnight on September 29, 2006.

Robin was already going cold in her arms. Across the street, a woman was screaming. And just before the woman and her bar could disappear, Ashley did something that she didn't remember doing before—but that she must've done, because that's how the potion worked. She couldn't change anything. She could only relive it. And yet, she saw something now that she swore she hadn't seen the first time around: the name of the bar. She saw it, just before it blinked out of existence and was replaced by a vacant lot.

Ashley Silver woke with a start, and reached to her nightstand for something to write on. For something to write *with*. But all she managed to do was knock something to the floor, something that shattered upon impact: the second vial of potion.

※ 4 ※

It would be a month before another batch of potion was ready. That's what Tracy had said. But as Ashley swept the the remains of the broken vial into a dustpan, she found she didn't much care. She didn't need the potion anymore, not now that she'd figured out the name of the bar. All she needed *now* was her phone, a search engine, and a bit of luck.

And for the first time in a good long while, it seemed that luck was on her side. Because though googling the name of the bar brought up way more hits than she'd expected—many of them archived City Directories from decades ago—it was surprisingly easy to track down where it was lurking these days.

"The Strumpet's Sister" read the review, "is a dive tucked into the basement of an upholsterer's warehouse on the banks of the Anacostia. And though many an establishment has shuttered just as quick as it's opened in this space, the Sister seems here to stay."

The Anacostia. Redheaded stepchild of the Potomac. Ashley smiled. All she had to do was get to Washington before Ada found an excuse to move it.

❦

SHE ROSE with the sun the next morning, determined to get a run in before her flight. And run she did: up Old Wharf, up Julien, up Hoyt, and up Bank. When she reached the center of town, she took a detour across Main Street and ran into the graveyard to say hello to her grandparents. But it was the briefest of greetings, and she trusted they'd understand why. She had work to do, and soon enough she was looping back home via Chatham Road.

Ashley was making her final descent down Deep Hole when she caught sight of Doris Brown, the family's longtime neighbor, perched on her porch like a nosy old bird. The poor wrinkled wretch had been living alone for years now, and she had nothing to do each day but to sit there and pass judgment upon the neighborhood—in between her occasional glances at the sea.

She peered out at the world from over the lip of a coffee mug she held close to her face with a pair of trembling hands. She stared through squinted eyes and tried to make sense of a world that had stopped making sense to her long ago. But whereas Doris would've frowned at the sight of any of the other Silvers, she was ready with nod and a smile for Ashley.

Ashley pulled the headphones from her ears and draped them around her neck. Then she strode across the lawn to give the old woman a kiss on the cheek. And it was only then that Ash realized how much the six miles had taken out of her, so she copped a squat on the grass to cool off.

"I haven't worked up a sweat like that in years," said Doris.

Ashley grinned. "Not even while watching your stories?"

Doris blushed, then laughed. "Fingers don't do the walking the way they used to," she said.

"They've got toys for that," said Ashley.

Doris raised an eyebrow. "Have they now?"

Ashley nodded. "Ryan bought me one once," she said, "to keep me company while he was away."

"My Ryan?" asked Doris, and she beamed for a second at the

memory of her grand-nephew's particular combination of kindness and lewdness—and at his utter lack of male fragility.

"Course I was still seeing Robin at the time, too," said Ashley, "but there were times when Ryan was off on a west coast swing at the same damn time Robin was in Europe. So his gift did come in handy every once in a while."

"So hard to believe he's gone," said Doris, her smile making way for a frown, the twinkle in her eye washed away by a tear.

"That they're *both* gone," said Ashley.

Doris set aside her coffee, then took hold of Ashley's face with her two shaking hands. "He *loved* you, child. I hope you know that. None of the girls he took up with could keep up with him, none till you. And that meant *everything* to my Ryan. First, that you tried at all. And then, that you succeeded."

Ashley smiled. But she knew that she only kept up with Ryan because he *let* her keep up. And she knew that he'd *let* her because he'd *loved* her. She knew *that* was the difference.

Ryan had loved her. A lot. But had she ever loved him enough in return? Ashley wasn't sure. After all, she wasn't about to confront a madwoman about *his* death. His death she seemed willing to let slide. Sure, his death was an accident, and what the hell was she going to do about it anyway? But why wasn't she as busted up about Ryan being gone as she was about Robin? They died one day after the other, for Christ's sake.

Did she love him less than she loved Robin? Or just differently?

Did she love *anyone*, for that matter? *Could* she? Maybe it just wasn't in her nature.

The phone strapped to her arm began to buzz, and Ashley sighed at the alarm—at the brutal and abrupt call back to reality.

"Your doohickey," said Doris, letting go of Ashley and pointing at the phone.

Ashley nodded and stood. Then, before she made her way

across the yard and into her family's home, she bent back down to offer Doris a final kiss, this one on her forehead.

"Be good," said Ashley.

"I will if you will," said Doris, flashing a saucy grin.

"No promises," said Ashley.

⚜

THEY'D GONE to Washington once, all three of them together: Ashley, Robin, and Ryan. Ryan had a game, Robin had a show, and Ashley had her pick of a half-dozen different clubs at which to dance. But their happiest moments, as always during those years, were the moments they spent together. Like the afternoon they'd spent getting lost in Arlington National Cemetery, for instance, which was what Ashley's cab was passing now.

Ash looked out the window of the taxi that was speeding her towards her destination, towards her revenge, and she remembered fondly the way she, her boyfriend, and her girlfriend had meandered through the rows of austere stones on their way to the memorial that had been their purpose in coming. She remembered herself wrapped around one of Ryan's massive arms, Robin wrapped around the other, and how they'd refused to stop for directions. Fallen leaves danced across the rolling green lawns as each of them pulled their hoodies tighter against their shivering bodies. High above them, oblivious to everything below, airliners thundered through the sky. They left trails of white in their wake, trails which stood in stark contrast against the darkening blue.

They cried together when they found what they were looking for, that monument of marble and bronze in section 46. It was near dusk, near time for the place to close, and they were trading stories about what they remembered from watching the space shuttle explode back when they were kids. Ryan's teacher had turned the TV off straight away, but Robin's hadn't. That old bitch had made them watch, had refused to take questions, and had demanded silence from the confused second graders. Ashley couldn't remember what she remembered. She was younger than the others, and anyway she was too busy running her hand over the embossed faces of the lost astronauts to have anything intelligent to say anyway.

And now, in the car years later, she thought about how selfish it was that she was going to use this opportunity she'd come across—the ability to travel through time—to do something as trivial as bring her lost love back to life. Shouldn't she be thinking bigger? What if she found her way back to 1986 instead, and warned them to call off the launch? What if she went back to 1963 and drove to the Texas School Book Depository to beat the shit out of Lee Harvey Oswald before he could take his shot at the president?

What if she went to 1889, to Austria, and smothered a certain dictator-to-be with a pillow? Isn't that the sort of thing you were supposed to do when you discovered time travel? Was undoing the death of your rock star girlfriend really enough? "With great power comes great responsibility"—that's what Spider-Man's Uncle Ben was famous for saying. And all that motherfucker could do was climb walls.

"We're here," said the cabbie, breaking Ashley from her reverie. And when she looked out the window and saw the building, she saw that he was right. And the sight of the building filled her with rage, that squat dive of a bar tucked into the basement of a ramshackle old warehouse. All thoughts of altruism or the greater good were gone, replaced by a thirst—perhaps unquenchable—for vengeance.

Ashley handed the cabbie the fare, plus a sizable tip, then got out of the car. A woman with a bouffant had just slipped in the front, a walking anachronism that confirmed that this was for sure the place.

"No time like the present," Ashley said to herself. And she would've laughed at the pun, probably would've fell down laughing at it at any other time, but this was no laughing matter. Not anymore.

☙❧

HEADS TURNED as she stepped into the bar, as if she were the one that was out of place. And she supposed the sweatpants and the hoodie could have been cause for that regardless of what bar she'd stepped into, and when, but she didn't care. She had one purpose here, and one purpose only: finding and catching Ada. And if that quest devolved into a chase, she didn't want to be caught in heels and a tight skirt. Sneakers and sweats were the name of the game here, no matter what kind of looks that got her.

Ashley ignored the gawking and turned her attention toward the bar, looking for a vaguely familiar face. She knew from Robin's stories that Ada was in charge of the place these days, and though she'd only seen Ada once from afar, she felt fairly certain she'd recognize the woman when she saw her.

What she hadn't expected was for Ada to give herself away. But that's just what she did. As soon as Ashley had turned to face the bar, a woman made a dash for the back door. And that made Ashley smile, because that had to be Ada. That just had to be.

Ashley gave chase to the woman who'd ruined her life, dodging and weaving through a crowd that seemed to be getting in the way at every possible moment: an elbow here, a head tossed back in laughter there. By the time Ashley reached the door through which her quarry had escaped, an eerie orange light flashed out from behind it. She threw herself into the heavy thing, shoulder-first, and stumbled out into a deserted alleyway. She looked around and found herself alone, alone save for a fading orange glow. It pulsed out at her from what looked a like a tear in the very air—a tear that seemed to be sewing itself shut with each passing moment.

Ashley ran for it and threw a hand into the hole to hold it

open, then both hands. But it was too much for her, the force with which the portal seemed determined to shut, and she didn't want to lose a hand—or two!—so she stepped back and let go. She let go and shouted "SHIT."

"Tough break," said someone lurking in the shadows.

Ashley whipped around to see where the voice was coming from, her eyes struggling to adjust to the darkness. She saw a loading dock, a stretch of pavement rolling down toward a river-bank, and a small skiff tied up at the water's edge, but no person at all—nothing from which a voice might have emerged. Then, finally, when it seemed she had spun around at least twice on the spot—maybe three times—she caught sight of a hooded figure lurking beneath the loading dock. And as the figure drew closer, their luminous green eyes came into view from within the shadows of the cowl. And Ashley felt like she might've been looking into a mirror, for those eyes were just like hers.

"Are you Ada?" asked Ashley.

"Tamson," said the figure as they drew nearer. Then they pointed at where the rip in the air had been. "Ada went that way."

"You a friend of hers?" asked Ashley.

Tamson laughed. "Hardly," they said. "In fact, our only connection is the man we both married."

Ashley's jaw dropped. *It couldn't be,* she thought. Another of her great-grandfather's seven wives was still alive? Nearly a hundred years later?

"If you'd be willing to hold these robes for me," said Tamson, "I could go after her."

Ashley raised an eyebrow. "You got something on underneath there?" she asked.

"Yes," said Tamson.

"And the robes are heavy or something?"

"Yes."

"You can't just take 'em off and drop 'em on the ground?" asked Ashley.

Tamson was close enough now that Ashley could see her smile. "Very good," said Tamson. "You didn't fall for it. Glad to see that you're smarter than I was."

"Are you Tamson O'Rourke?" asked Ashley. "My great-grandfather's first wife?"

Tamson nodded. Then, finally, she pushed back her cowl.

She was beautiful, if a bit gaunt, her red hair just as vibrant as it was in the stories that had been passed down over the years—albeit far more tousled, far more of a mess. But the smile that she'd been famous for? It seemed as if Tamson only had the one smile she'd given already, and that was it. The look on her face now was that of a broken woman.

"You can't take the robes off at all?" asked Ashley.

Tamson shook her head in a silent no. "Someone must wear them. The job is too important."

"The job?" said Ashley. "What's the job?"

Tamson snorted back a laugh. "You wouldn't believe me if I told you."

Ashley wasn't so sure about that, given everything she'd been through, but she decided to take Tamson at her word. "I'd offer to take over for you," said Ashley, "give you a rest, but..." She trailed off and shook a thumb at the spot where Ada had escaped through.

"You've got a life left to live," said Tamson with a nod.

"So," said Ashley, turning to face Ada's escape hatch, "any idea how to open this thing again?"

"The Veil?" said Tamson.

Ashley nodded, running her hands through the air as if she might find an edge at which to tug—as if this so-called "veil" were like a Christmas present sealed up tight with tape, or a scab she could pull off with one determined yank (if only she could find the one frayed edge).

"You don't want to go that way," said Tamson.

Ashley gave an exasperated sigh. "And why not?" she said.

"The Veil," said Tamson, "is like the potion you drank—"

Ashley was about to say "Wait a second" and ask how Tamson knew about that, but Tamson pressed on.

"It can only take you were your blood has been. But," said Tamson, "if you're willing to wander the halls of the Sister instead, you can get just about anywhere you want to go. You just have to be willing to open enough doors."

"Well," said Ashley, pointing toward where the veil was supposed to be, "my blood has been near her blood, for the whole of the time she was married to my great-grandfather. So that's good enough for me."

"True enough," said Tamson, then she set a cold hand upon Ashley's shoulder—cold enough that she felt it through the hoodie, and gave a shiver in response. "But you aren't going after her just to stay and chat, are you?"

"No," said Ashley, and for the first time she spoke aloud her true purpose: "I'm going to kill her."

"But you can't," said Tamson. "Not back then. Because that's not what happened."

"Fine," said Ashley, shrugging off Tamson's hand—partly out of annoyance and partly out of discomfort. "Then I'll just get the answers out of her that I need, and I'll watch my great-grandfather kill her instead. After all," said Ashley, "*that* happened, didn't it?"

Tamson nodded. "He killed her yes, but you never spoke to her."

"How do you know?"

"Because I was there the first time you spoke to her," said Tamson, "and it was *that* way." She pointed to the door that led back inside.

Ashley stalked off in frustration, then kicked a garbage can for good measure.

"I'm sorry," said Tamson.

"When did you see us?" asked Ashley, turning on the spot to confront Tamson again. "Which door will take me there?"

"I don't know," she said. "I wish I could tell you."

"You just expect me to wander and wander until I find her?" spat Ashley. "I don't have time for that."

"In there," said Tamson, pointing at the bar's back door one more time, "you have all the time in the world."

Ashley stared at the door. *Maybe*, she thought. Maybe it was true that time worked differently inside this place. That was certainly true when Robin stepped into a bar in New Orleans in 2003 and walked out a few drinks later in 2005. But even if she did have all the *time* in the world, Ashley didn't have nearly as much patience.

Tamson gave a little *ahem* to break Ash from her reverie, then asked "What are you after? What are you after *really*?"

Ashley didn't know what to say. Answers were in short supply, too. And though Tracy had asked her essentially the same thing just last night, she wasn't sure she believed what she'd said anymore. Was this *just* about seeing Robin's face again? Or was there something more to it than that?

Tamson was at Ashley's shoulder again, but she didn't set a hand upon Ash this time. She simply spoke. "Go in," she said. "Ada's in there somewhere. And your answer might be, too."

Ashley cast a sidelong glance at Tamson, though she wasn't sure why. And perhaps it was because she was struggling for something to say, for some way to say goodbye and make her farewell— perhaps it was because of that that Ashley brought up what she brought up next.

"We have the same eyes," Ashley told her ancestor's first wife. "But I suppose I shouldn't be surprised," she said. "Everyone's always told me that I have the same eyes as my great-grand-mother, and they all said the way she won my great-grandfather's heart was because she looked like you, his first love."

Tamson looked surprised by this. "She did?"

Ashley turned a bit more, so that they were face to face and she didn't have to strain her neck any longer. "Yep," she said. "That's how the story's been passed down."

"What was her name?" asked Tamson.

"You've never met her," said Ashley, gesturing toward the boat, "in all your travels?"

Tamson looked desperate, and now her hands were back on Ashley's shoulders—as if to hold Ash in place until she got her answer. "The name?"

Ashley thought about walking away just to spite the woman, just to play her favorite role: the most difficult person in the room. But something in Tamson's eyes—those eyes that felt *so* familiar—something in her eyes said that she was as desperate for this name as Ashley was to see Robin again. Ashley knew that look, that wanton desperation. She'd seen it in the mirror that very morning.

"Her name was Annie," said Ashley. "Annie O'Reilly."

Tamson let go, and let go a deep exhale of breath she seemed to have been holding onto since last she'd spoken. She looked as if she was trying to commit the name to memory.

"You got a pen?" asked Ashley. "I can write it down."

"I can carry nothing with me," said Tamson, "nothing that I wasn't carrying when I took the robes into my arms."

"You need a new job," said Ashley, managing a weak smile to go along with her weak joke.

Tamson nodded, then turned to begin the walk back toward her skiff.

Ashley shouted after her. "You aren't going to wish me good luck?" she said.

Tamson stopped and looked at Ashley from over her shoulder. "We both have places to be," said Tamson, then she continued on her way.

Ashley nodded to herself, then turned to open the door.

She couldn't change what happened. That was true. But what happened could still change her.

Because every time she went looking for Robin, or for Ada—every time she made that her mission—*every time*, Ashley got distracted. She'd see a person she *swore* was one of them, she'd see that person dashing through a door, and Ashley would give chase. But she'd never catch them. No. And then she'd end up in one predicament or another instead.

And oh, the people she met along the way...

IT WASN'T Helen's face that launched a thousand ships, because it is never the face. The face is but a promise made by the body. And a promise might launch a dozen ships, perhaps two, but it is only a promise fulfilled that will make men go to war.

Or a promise broken.

What Ashley taught Helen, the future queen of Sparta—the future princess of Troy—was the same thing she'd taught good ol' Anne Boleyn a few days before (or thousands of years later, depending on your perspective). "You must make them work for it," Ash told each woman. "You *must*. But then, when they've done the work, you must deliver."

"But how?" they each asked her, and she watched them shiver in the shadows where they took her counsel—the shadow of a mother who'd survived the passions of gods, the shadow of a sister who had seduced kings. But Ashley did not tell them. No, she showed them instead.

In a bedchamber outside her father's city, Helen and Ashley shared the cock of a slave Ash stole from the house of a swine-herd—a master of pigs who imagined himself a bigger tyrant than his station would ever allow. The women passed the poor boy's prick between themselves until he felt very rich indeed, and Ashley showed Helen how to handle the boy the way he handled his master's hogs: with a firm grip, but not so firm that the slip-pery beast slipped through the fingers. As she fumbled him towards ecstasy, Ashley assured Helen that all it would take was practice. And when Helen asked what she might do with the evidence each time she studied, when she asked Ashley what to do with the mess each man leaves behind, well of course Ash showed her.

While Helen stole back to her castle, Ashley showed the boy how to steal himself away from his master. She showed him the way to leave that place for good. She taught him how to roam the thousand halls of the Strumpet's Sister and find himself a life without chains. It was the least she could do, the literal *least*.

While Helen's desire was to outshine her mother through sheer force of will, Anne was quite content to use her place in the shadows to her advantage. And she told Ashley as much when they met.

She was nervous, having watched her sister—King Francis'

"English mare"—ride one French stallion after another. One after another, until she'd mounted the grandest steed of them all. And Anne was still more nervous now, watching her sister seduce their own sovereign. Mary used the tricks they'd learned together in that court across the sea, yes—tricks they'd learned *together*—but Anne knew that her hands were not as nimble as her sister's. Nor her hips, nor her mouth. She would never compare. She could never compete. Her thighs were stronger perhaps, strong enough that she would not be thrown off once seated. But how to be invited to sit—that was the question. How might she invite the invitation?

And so, Ashley danced for her. She taught Anne to play the game of chambers and antechambers in the only way she knew how. And when Ash's teasing became too much for Anne, when there was naught but the fine linen of a smock between one woman's skin and the other's, Ashley reminded Anne what she'd said about the difference between promises and promises fulfilled.

Ashley straddled her then, so wet herself that Anne must've felt it through the cloth as her stomach pressed against Ashley with each hurried breath.

"And what have I promised you?" said Ashley, her hands on Anne's neck, her thumbs stroking Anne's trembling face.

"What *haven't* you promised?" said Anne.

Ashley nodded once, then slid her hands from Anne's neck to either side of the smock's neckline, taking hold of the fabric. She let Anne breathe against her once more, and then again—let Anne wonder what she was about to do, let her *imagine*—and then, when Ash was sure Anne had taken mental note of her technique, Ash tore that thing in half. The fabric split down the middle and fell away from Anne, and she seemed stunned by the violence of it—even if she'd known it was coming. Anne's chest heaved, her bare skin blushing as Ashley rode the wave of her shuddering form, sliding her own slick groin from belly to breast to mark it as her own.

"And yet," said Anne, panting, "this is still just a promise."

"But the voracious," said Ashley, "like *you*, like the men you desire—they must be promised much."

"And I must give them more?" asked Anne, her hands on Ashley's ass now to hold her still.

"Indeed," said Ashley, and then she showed Anne how to make two hands feel like three. Like four. How to make a lover certain —*so* certain—that her body was no longer just one body, but a host unto itself.

It would help for a while, the things Ashley taught her. Ash even dared to hope that it might help her for longer than it was supposed to. But then she went back to check, and she was there in the crowd when they took Anne's head from her.

For a promise she made and could not keep.

FOR A WHILE THEN, Ashley decided just to watch. If she couldn't change anything, then she wouldn't even try.

She hid inside a closet at Bing Crosby's to see if presidents, like gentlemen, prefer blondes. And while Marilyn scratched Jack's seven-year itch, Ashley let her fingers have some fun of their own.

She watched while Mary Godwin gave herself to Percy Shelley, watched as he took her from behind while she leaned upon her mother's gravestone for support. And Ashley was having herself a ménage à moi when she spied across the way, from her shelter in the sanctum, someone else watching. She couldn't be sure, because her eyesight was only so-so, but she would've bet money it was Mary's mum. Her skirts weren't lifted or anything, not like Ashley's just then—it was nothing so kinky as that—but it looked like she was smiling, like she was happy to see her daughter happy.

After that, Ash went to sea for a while.

She watched Anne Bonny and Mary Read strip the clothing off themselves, each trying to prove to the other what they really were underneath—underneath the breeches they wore—even though Bonny knew who Read was already, and Read Bonny, and all that they were really revealing were the parts they each had to play with.

When they were done playing with each other's parts and back to playing their parts above decks, Ashley took Bonny aside and told her how she'd seen the cap'n looking at Read, told her that she best let the skipper in on the secret. Ashley told Bonny she best let Cap'n Rackham know the truth about ol' Mark Read before Rackham slit the throat of the person he saw now only as "the other man."

Ash hung with them for a while, hung with them until just before they were destined to hang. She went home to 2007 for a second and spent a night in the bar googling, trying to figure out what she could do. Was there anything she could do?

Both Bonny and Read pled the belly to buy themselves time, and both were offered stays of execution until they gave birth, but Read didn't make it. That's what Ashley learned from her phone that night. Read caught a fever hotter than hell and her jailers joked, pointing down at the ground beneath their feet—at the damnation they imagined below them—that Read's fever was just a taste of things to come.

Nothing was certain about what happened to Bonny, though. So Ashley read until daybreak about where and when she was last seen, then she rushed back through the door she'd kept ajar and got to work.

Ashley never found her, though. But she hoped someone had, that someone might. Someday.

AFTER THAT, she stayed away from the tragic stuff for a bit. It was a chore, because the saddest denouements were preceded by the hottest intermezzos, but she was worn out. She'd lived through enough tragedy for a lifetime.

Maybe two.

And so, she fucked the Chairman of the Board just to see if Ava Gardner was right about that 110 pounder having 10 pounds of cock. And though she didn't have a tape measure handy, Ashley's cervix would've signed a sworn affidavit in support of good ol' Ava if only she'd given it a pen.

Ashley and John Lennon had themselves a drunken roll atop a pile of coats while Yoko entertained downstairs. Ash slipped out just after John slipped out of her, but she had no idea he was going to fall asleep as soon as she was gone. It wasn't until the partygoers were all standing by the door, waiting to say their goodbyes, and Ash asked someone what was the hold-up—it wasn't until then that she realized what she'd done.

She would've hung around to collect her coat—it was a nice coat, a dark blue Levi's trucker jacket she'd had with her since a trip to the 60s, the kind with the cream-colored Sherpa collar— yeah, she would have hung around for it, because she loved that thing, but she couldn't stop laughing and she had to get out of there. It was 1973, and yet she had a Lil' Kim lyric stuck in her head.

She'd jumped on the dick and rode his ass to sleep.

But Ashley couldn't sing that song now. She was 23 years too early.

After that, after the laughter, it was more fun than ever for a while. She waited for Tenzing Norgay at the bottom of Everest in 1953 and asked if he had a mountain for *her* to climb. She caught the sixteenth Louis' eye, just to sneak around Versailles. Then she leapt forward to get drunk with Wilde and his green fairy. She tried—half-heartedly, given her lack of success to this point—to lure him home with her, to a place where his depravity would not only be accepted but *celebrated*. But he laughed, swore her visions were an invention borne only of absinthe, and she gave up.

She snuck onto a ship bound for Australia, the Planter, just to see if she could fuck her way up from the keel to the cabins in six months or less. And once sexing up sailboats wasn't enough of a challenge, she roamed Rome for a bit, bouncing between bacchanalia until she'd come before Caligula on a vessel so absent of virtue that it was said Neptune himself sank it to the bottom of the sea.

Drunk on the power of her pussy, Ashley traveled the world. She sauntered from Babylon to Tenochtitlan and everywhere in between, to see if maybe—and yeah, she felt stupid even thinking this—she could become what so many dudes had already called her: a goddess.

She never gave a name when they asked for one, because she was pretty sure there'd never been a Cult of Ashley, but none of the names they gave her sounded familiar either. Then again: she'd been a C student in Ancient Civ, so what did she know?

Once, she went as far back as she could, as deep into the labyrinthine halls of the Strumpet's Sister as was possible. And there she found a door made of stone and not wood—not a polished portal by any means, but instead the crudest of openings.

She stepped out into a mostly dried river bed. Then she followed the trickle of water she found there until it became a stream, until it became a river that disappeared into as lush an oasis as she'd ever seen.

A man staggered from behind a bush at the edge of the garden, as if he'd just learned to walk, and he stopped dead in his tracks at the sight of her. Ashley had worn the simplest cloth she could find, prepared to abandon even that if she made it back far enough, but she didn't think it was the sight of her clothes that shocked him. She felt fairly certain, in that moment, that this man had never seen a woman before.

It couldn't have been *him*, she thought, not *the* first human of all—it literally couldn't have been, because anyone old enough to have taken sex ed knew that the first must've been a woman, right?—but Ashley still found herself wondering if it could be. Could it be him?

She held a hand to her chest, and because she never—not *ever*—passed up the chance to fuck with someone, she introduced herself as Lilith. Because she sure as shit was never going to be someone's Eve.

He held his hand to his chest, but said nothing. He was waiting for her to tell him. And it was then that it occurred to her: he was all alone, so he didn't need a name.

He tapped his hand against his chest again and shook his chin at her, as if to say "C'mon. Lay it on me."

And of course—of *course*—the first name that came to her for this man, this maybe-just-maybe *first* man, was the name of *her* first man.

Ashley pointed at him and said "Adam."

☙❧

ASHLEY TOOK a break then and spent some time with Dickinson in her garden. Emily let Ashley read her letters to Gilbert before she put them in the mail, let Ash read Gilbert's letters back when they came. And as she showed Ash how to tend to a thing without killing it—something Ashley had never quite mastered—they debated the difference between affection and eros, between eros and romance.

Then Ashley got the hell out of there before she fell into bed with Emily, too.

☙❧

THE LAST DOOR she opened brought her to a hospital in Hyannis in 1944, and this adventure wasn't about sex at all. It didn't take her long to realize she was about to see the end of a story she'd been told, over and over, since she was a kid. She took a seat next to a sharp-dressed soldier in the hallway, outside a door marked "S. SILVER," but Ashley didn't think twice about trying to pull the dude into a linen closet to thank him for his service.

Once maybe, but not twice.

Behind the closed door to S. SILVER's room, voices were rising. The soldier asked if Ashley was family.

She smiled at him. "I hope not," she said, but when he looked confused by her flirting she told him "Yes, I'm family with *them*. But it's a distant connection."

"I'm here on behalf the Army," he told her. "Your relation over there—" he nodded at the door "—is a vet, and he's asked to be buried in his uniform."

Ashley took note of the folded clothes in the soldier's lap. "Looks pretty old."

The soldier smiled and nodded his chin at the door again. "*He's* pretty old."

A familiar voice shouted behind the door, a voice Ashley hadn't heard since she was fifteen years old. "All she wants," said her grandfather, "is to be next to Mum. It doesn't have to be—"

But what *it* was and what it didn't have to be—that was cut off by a cackle even more cutting than the one Grampy described when he told the story. And then came the voice she'd long longed to hear. "You'd sooner catch a weasel asleep," shouted her great-grandfather, "than convince me to allow that strumpet's corpse to pollute the eternal resting place of *my* family."

"I should never have come," said Grampy, and his voice was clearer now, though not as loud—as if he'd moved to the door. "Dot thought that age might have softened you," he said. "But I can see, even after a century spent on this Earth, you're still a no good son of a bitch."

The door to Silas' room swung open and slammed against the wall inside the room.

"I would live a hundred years more," Silas screamed at his retreating son, at that handsome man Ashley never thought she'd see again. "I would live a hundred years more if only to see that the two of you never tarnish my family's good name."

Grampy stopped at the threshold, his back to his father, and stared at the wall just above Ashley's head. There were tears in his eyes, this man who was a few years younger than she was at this point, and she wanted to hold him close and tell him it was okay, that it would kill him to hold it in. But he had already sniffled and called the sadness back into himself.

He was halfway down the hall when his father screamed, though the phlegm that was nearly suffocating him, "A PLAGUE ON BOTH YOUR HOUSES!"

Ashley and the soldier looked at each other then. "Would you like to go first?" he asked her. "I can wait."

Ash nodded and stood. And as she smoothed the front of her skirt, she nodded at the soldier and bid him farewell.

Once Ashley had reached the threshold, her great-grandfather turned to face her. "And who might you be?" he asked as he squinted, as he tried to make out her face through the cataracts and whatever else was working to blind those milky eyes of his.

Ashley leaned in close, until she was sure he could see the eyes she'd long been told were her inheritance from his side of the family. The same eyes that had belonged to the love of his life. And not just one love, but *loves* plural.

"I," she told him, "am the plague upon your house."

Then she reached between his legs to see if the rumors were true, to see if her eyes had cast the same spell as those who had come before. And then—finding that yes, the rumors were correct—she wrapped her fist around that weakest part of that very weak man, and she squeezed until he yelped.

Then she squeezed some more.

And it wasn't until the soldier came to the door that Ashley let go. The old man had passed out anyway.

THAT AFTERNOON, before she made her way back inside the bar to be done with her traveling once and for all, she took a stroll through the Cape Cod of yore. And it was at the end of this excursion that she caught sight of the soldier one last time. He was having a drink with a frail-looking woman inside the Sister, inside the very place she was headed.

Ashley paused for a moment, not sure what to do next, not sure if she should risk bumping into someone who might prolong her exit and her return to reality. She sighed, thinking *I could see myself with a guy like that.* After all she'd been through, it would be a nice change of pace to *not* be the strong one in a relationship. Then the frail-looking woman laughed at some joke the soldier had made and turned her head so that Ashley could see her face for the first time.

In her mind, Ashley could see herself with a guy like that. And then she *did.* When the woman turned her head so that Ashley could see her face, Ash did indeed see herself with a guy like that.

The frail woman—she was Ashley, an Ashley that was yet to come.

"How?" Ashley said to herself. And though a bustling street and a wall of brick and windows stood between them, the Ashley that was yet to come seemed to hear the Ashley of right now as she spoke. For a moment, across the distance that stood between them—both the yards and the years—the two women locked eyes.

And it was then that something inside of Ashley's brain broke, and she fell unconscious on the spot.

❧ II ❧
CAN'T GET YOU OUT OF MY HEAD

2008–2011

❧ 6 ❧

When Ashley woke, it was to the sound of waves lapping gently against the side of wherever it was that she was resting. She blinked her eyes open and found herself staring up at a canopy of stars, a beauty obstructed only by the hooded figure who stood above her. And though a part of her felt as though she should be screaming with fright at this moment, the rest of her felt at peace—as if she'd been here before and she knew, just *knew*, that everything was going to be okay.

And it was that thought which brought everything back to her, the reality of her situation. She *had* been here before. Or, rather, the frail future version of her had. But now, somehow, the once and future Ashleys were one and the same. That look they'd shared in 1944—that had been the cause of it.

Ash sat bolt upright, rocking the boat. And though she half-expected the ferryman to grunt in disapproval, she didn't. Because she hadn't. She never had.

Ashley felt a pain stab through her skull, from one temple to the next and back again, as if someone were trying to crack her open to feast on the meat inside her head. It was one thing to travel through the past and know how things were going to turn out. It was another thing altogether to walk through the present and know what was going to happen before it did.

"We're almost there," said the ferryman.

Ashley was about to ask where 'there' was, but she knew the answer before she could ask the question. Nevertheless, she turned her attention to the figure looming above her, the cloaked person who was punting them along the Potomac, and asked the question anyway.

When the ferryman didn't answer that query, Ashley offered up another. "Do you remember me?" she asked.

The ferryman looked down at Ashley—took a good, hard look —then said, "We haven't met yet."

"In the alley," said Ashley. "A few months ago?" she added. "You don't remember?"

"A few months ago for you," said the ferryman, "may be a few months from *now* for me. Or a few years."

While Ash puzzled over that most peculiar statement, the ferryman turned the boat towards the Anacostia. And it wasn't until she caught sight of the Sister's back alley that Ashley realized what might be about to happen. It wasn't until she saw the figure of a voluptuous barmaid waiting for them at the water's edge that Ashley remembered what the ferryman had said to her however long ago.

I was there the first time you spoke to her, and it was that way. That's what the ferryman had said, before pointing toward the time-traveling building Ashley had wandered through for weeks now. Months, even.

"Her" being the barmaid smiling wickedly at them as they made their approach. "Her" being *Ada*.

All the old anger welled up inside Ashley. And before she could think to stop herself, she said aloud "I'm going to kill her."

But then, inside her head, a small but confident voice uttered a single word: *Nope*.

The ferryman tossed a rope to Ada, once they were close enough, and Ada made quick work of pulling the boat out of the water and up the smooth incline of the launch.

And though perhaps Ada's strength should've given Ashley pause—or else the voice she'd heard utter its definitive *Nope*—Ashley sprung from the skiff anyway, the moment they were clear of the water, and tackled Ada to the ground.

After she'd landed her first few punches, Ashley cast a glance over her shoulder to see if the ferryman would intervene. But the hooded waif did nothing but stand there and watch.

Unfortunately for Ashley, this one moment of letting up was all it took for Ada to regain control of the situation. Ashley saw stars as she fell off of Ada, clutching at the temple where the old villainess had landed a blow of her own. And before Ash knew it, Ada was standing above her with a pistol aimed straight at her head.

Ada cocked the hammer of the old gun and smiled. "It would be a waste of a bullet," she said, "but you Silvers do aggravate me so."

Ashley wanted to say something tough just then, something some big screen hero would say in a moment like this. But as she stared down the barrel of Ada's six-shooter, Ashley realized she didn't want to die. Her heart was all aflutter, her bare arms and legs covered in a cold sweat. She wasn't ready. That's the thought that kept circling through her mind—circling and circling and circling, as she watched Ada lick blood from a split lip. *I'm not ready*, she thought. *I'm not ready*.

And then she remembered: this wasn't her time. She still had to get back to the soldier in the 40s. She still had to get *there* before she died. And that's why Ada said that shooting her would be a waste of a bullet: because Ada *knew*—must have known—

that Ashley wasn't going to die yet. So, even if she shot at Ash, Ada was going to miss.

Ashley pushed herself up off the ground. And though Ada made a show of raising her weapon, she didn't pull the trigger.

"What are you doing?" said Ada

Ashley took a step forward, right towards Ada's outstretched arm. She let the cold metal of the gun's barrel press into the warm flesh of her chest.

"I could kill you," said Ada, bluffing. "Right here and right now."

"I thought you said it would be a waste," said Ashley, staring the other woman dead in the eyes.

Ada grimaced, her finger itchy on the trigger. "I've wasted a lot more than bullets in my life," she said.

They stood there for a minute then, then a minute more, neither of them moving a muscle until the sound of the ferryman's footsteps brought an end to their staring contest.

"Do you have what I asked for?" said Ada to the ferryman.

The ferryman nodded, then Ashley scoffed.

"I thought you couldn't carry anything," she said.

The ferryman nodded toward her skiff. "The boat carried it."

Ada lowered her gun. Then she strode down the embankment to collect whatever it was she'd tasked the ferryman with collecting for her.

What she returned with was a brown padded envelope, which she tossed at Ashley with a shout of "Catch." And it was as Ashley fumbled to keep the thing from dropping that Ada strode by and began to search the air of the alleyway for her hidden getaway.

"Word to the wise," said Ada, gun in one hand while she tore open a hole in the air with the other, "stop looking for me. Stop looking for Robin. There are consequences," she said, nodding at the package that was now firmly in Ashley's hands.

And then, in a flash of orange light, Ada was gone.

"Are you going to open it?" asked the ferryman, reminding Ashley that she was still there.

Ash nodded and tore open the package. Then she stared down at the gift she'd been given. She stared at it for a good, long while before the tears came, before she mumbled to herself "I can't fucking believe it."

The ferryman hovered over her shoulder, then asked "You can't believe what?"

It was a VHS tape in a too-big box, something vintage—from way back when video cassettes were new, and manufacturers packaged them up in big plastic cradles before wrapping them in cardboard.

Or did they just do that for porn?, Ashley wondered. She couldn't remember. She didn't *want* to.

On the cover of the box, a brunette woman knelt before a priest. With her back to the camera, she knelt like a child in prayer—though there was nothing remotely childlike about her.

She wore nothing but a string of rosary beads, which she'd hung around her small waist like a belt. And speaking of belts: her hands were on the belt of the priest, making to unbuckle it. And though one might think he'd be giving this blasphemous sight his full attention, maybe even imploring her to stop, he wasn't paying any attention to the brunette at all. His eyes faced forward. They looked straight at the camera—straight up at a leering Ashley—as he held a Bible in one hand and made the sign of the cross with the other.

In big, bold letters positioned to cover up the crack of the woman's ass, was the title: *Come, All Ye Faithful*. Below that, in a smaller typeface, the subtitle proclaimed that this was "the shocking conclusion to the trilogy which began with *Come Together* and *Come on Eileen*."

The ferryman asked Ashley what it was about the tape that was making her cry.

Ashley, in her lousy approximation of a British accent, asked: "Is that really what my hair looks like from the back?"

"Huh?" said the ferryman.

Ashley thought then of time-traveling Hermione Granger in *The Prisoner of Azkaban*, standing at the edge of the forest behind Hagrid's hut and watching a scene play out that she'd already lived through.

The ferryman laid a frail finger upon the box, pointing at the woman kneeling there. "Is that you?"

Ashley nodded.

"You're kneeling naked before a man of the cloth," said the ferryman, "about to do god-knows-what to him, and your *hair* is what you're worried about?"

Ashley coughed out a mirthless laugh. "Do you *see* how high they've teased that shit up? I mean, it was the 80s, but for Christ's sake."

The ferryman said nothing.

"It's not my hair that's bugging me," said Ashley to the ferryman.

"So," said the ferryman, "what is it?"

"My dad," said Ashley. "My dad rented this tape once."

❧

SHE'D FILMED the whole trilogy over the course of a long weekend, with a shady production company that had "acquired the rights" to film in an abandoned church that was set to be demolished on Monday morning. And it wasn't until the last scene on her third three-scene day in a row that Ashley admitted to herself that she'd taken on too much.

She rubbed at the swollen, achy mound between her legs and almost laughed at the thought that entered her head just then. *Is this*, she thought to herself, *the hill I'm going to die on?*

But she didn't laugh. She couldn't. Because the rubbing wasn't working and she didn't even have the strength to lift a hand to her mouth to lick it. She asked for lube, please and thank you, and closed her eyes. And she was deep into a daydream filled with bubble bath and bubble tea when a small plastic something fell onto her belly and broke her reverie. It rolled off her stomach and onto the hard wood of the pew, then plunked onto the floor.

Ashley opened her eyes and surveyed a scene so blasphemous it would've been orgasmic on any other day. Three men crowded around her: Strom, the old cameraman, who was twisting his wiry orange-gray beard around his index finger; John, the toothpick lighting guy who Strom looked like he wanted to strangle; and her co-star, Gideon, the kid playing the priest, who was stroking his half-flaccid cock and grunting like a pig as he paced between altar and pew.

She had no idea who had so unceremoniously dropped the bottle of lube onto her stomach. But, if she had to guess, she would have guessed it was Strom. He'd been giving Ash the evil eye since the day they'd cast her out of nowhere, instead of any of the girls he'd worked with before—the *professionals*—who knew what was what and how shit was done.

And Ashley was pretty sure he smirked at her as she gathered the strength to sit up and collect the bottle of Astroglide.

"So," said John, "we're decided then."

"Indeed," said Strom. "Doggie, reverse cowgirl, pile driver."

Gideon oinked his approval.

But Ash raised her hand, an affectation that made Gideon oink once more, and she asked "Wasn't that what we did this morning?"

Strom groaned. "No," he said. "That was doggie, cowgirl, missionary."

"Doesn't matter if it was the same," said Gideon, clutching the shaft of his penis so tightly this time that it turned a brilliant shade of puce. "Different weiner this time," he said. "It'll look totally different."

Ashley couldn't tell if he was kidding, or not. And, in a way, it was endearing. She had never, in all her travels, fucked someone that stupid before.

"Besides," said John, lifting Ashley's chin with this thumb and forefinger, "sweetheart, you look great when you're arching your back in this light."

"Fucking phenomenal," said Gideon.

Ashley sighed. "I just don't want to do the same old shit," she said. And she didn't. She'd seen her share of porn. She knew what turned her on, and what absolutely did not. And she knew that trying to make a *good* adult film in the early 80s would be as hard as beating the second quest in *Zelda*, but she also knew that she just *had* to try.

Ashley cast a glance toward the altar, hoping for a little help from her director, but he was passed out—*coked* out, in fact—and he wasn't going to be any help. The success of his last two films had gone to his head, apparently by way of his red-as-Rudolph's nose.

She tried to tell the rest of them that Jepp wanted the film to be special, but Strom just rolled his eyes. "Jepp is gacked out of his mind right now," he said. "So why don't you let us worry about what this film is or isn't? Mm'kay?"

And Ashley was too tired to argue, so she laid back down and waited for whatever was next.

What was next, it turned out, was a request from Gideon. He moved around to the side of the pew were Ashley's head was resting and gave his limp dick a slap as he asked "You mind?"

The fluffer was gone for the day, so she didn't see what choice she had. She scooched herself toward him and let her head fall backwards over the edge of the bench, her hair long enough now that it brushed against the hard wood floor. Then she clamped her eyes shut and opened her mouth wide.

As he guided himself in, Ash heard Strom shout "Hey, waita-minute! We should be rolling on this!"

She relaxed her throat and did her best not to gag. And though part of the deal she'd made with herself when setting out on this particular adventure was that she would never drift out of the moment, that she would never let herself become some simple meat puppet, she turned herself over to them entirely this time. She'd never tried *that*, after all. She'd never tried to just not try.

When Gideon tweaked her nipples, she barely felt it. And, later, when he drove himself into her, it felt like nothing more than a vague dream.

She screamed when she was supposed to, squealed when she was supposed to, and called out to God as if only He could save her from this exquisite defiling. When it was time to switch positions, she let them pull her strings. And when the priest spilled his seed on her face, like he was Onan and she was just an extension of the filthy ground she knelt upon, she did not flinch. She did not move at all.

In the end, Ashley wasn't sure how long she'd been kneeling there—by herself, with her eyes closed, and the camera's eye closed too—before somebody finally tossed her a towel.

⚜

WHEN SHE WAS YOUNG, Ashley's dad was in charge on the weekends. Mum was working every damn Saturday and Sunday, struggling to build her pediatric practice from the ground up, so she turned to her husband to play the part of Mister Mom.

And he did a great job, Ashley recalled, even if he wasn't the most inventive parent in the world. Their Sunday pilgrimages to Landmark Video in Lowell were all Ash really wanted out of life anyway. The chance to pick out a new cassette of cartoons every weekend, one of her own that she didn't have to share with her brother, that was *everything* back then. And Landmark had the best selection around.

The biggest adult section too, it turned out, though she wouldn't realize that for a while.

She never paid much attention to the dark corner of the store that her dad disappeared into while she stalked the stacks deciding between He-Man and She-Ra, nor while she followed her brother on the sly and tried to catch him looking at something he shouldn't. But when she went back into the store later, as an adult, Ashley was struck by the fact that there wasn't a curtain dividing the two rooms from each other. Anyone could wander in there, and it wasn't like they had a clerk to spare to check IDs at the threshold. The place was too damn busy for that. They'd hung a hand-made sign with a piece of scotch tape as a deterrent, and left it at that.

Every case out on the floor of the store was empty—both the kid-friendly stuff and the adult fare—so you had to grab a dull stubby pencil and a scrap of paper to write down the numbers of the videos you wanted. That's what made it possible for her dad to grab his "daddy movies" from the same counter where she and Michael would pick up their own stuff. The clerk always asked Dad if he wanted separate bags, but there was no judgment there. Dad wasn't anything special. There were lots of marriages in those days that shouldn't have been marriages anymore, and his was a generation distrustful of shrinks. They were too cheap to pay a therapist what they were worth anyway, so they all learned to self-soothe.

Ashley's dad, Robin's dad—*everyone's* dad back then. Probably their moms, too. Why else did they watch *Dirty Dancing* so damn often?

Once they got home, Ashley and Michael knew the drill. Their movies were for later on, when Mummy came back from work. Until then, the kids were to play outside. They were not to knock on the windows or try to peek between the heavy brown curtains their dad had drawn closed inside. They were not to snoop at the door to hear if he was listening to another Eddie

Murphy special, like the one he and their uncle had let the kids listen to from the other room on the day that Mummy and Auntie had their tubes tied and the dads were left in charge. If they had to use the bathroom, they were to go in through the side door, use the toilet upstairs, and not to disturb Daddy while they did it. They were not to open the door to the downstairs under any circumstances. If they asked him why he got 4 movies and they each only got 1, he would tell them to mind their own business. But that was the only time he ever got angry at them. In every other way, their father was the dream dad. A patient listener, he was quick with a joke and almost always available as a shoulder to cry on. But the Saturday routine was the Saturday routine. And that was that.

That was that, until the one day that it wasn't.

The sun was coming down and he still hadn't opened the door and called the kids in for dinner. Ashley and Michael were sitting on the edge of the porch, their eyes on the road, worried that Mummy was going to get home and they were still going to be outside and Daddy was going to get in trouble because of that.

Or, well, Ashley was worried.

Michael was lost in his own world, still doodling in his sketchbook. And that's why it was Ash who leapt to her feet at the sight of Mummy's red car speeding past the neighbors—the neighbors whose house was between theirs and the street. That's why it was Ashley who found the spare key hidden beneath the green ash tray, the one they were only supposed to use in case of emergencies. That's why it was she who found her dad passed out on the couch with a hand down his pants. The TV was snowy with static, a tape was half-sticking out of the VCR, and the case was sitting open on the living room table.

Ashley grabbed the tape from the VCR, shoved it into the white plastic of the case, then snapped it shut. And it was as she was stuffing it back into the black plastic of the Landmark bag that she caught a glimpse of the cover, a cover she would never forget: the pretty girl with her back to the camera who was helping the priest get dressed even before she got dressed herself. Ashley shook her head and wondered why boys were just so freaking lazy.

Daddy stirred then and Ashley almost yelped in surprise. But she didn't. And he didn't wake up, not entirely. Ash ran outside, closed the door as lightly as she could, and sat down beside her brother. Her brother who was—yes, *of course* he was—still doodling.

Their mom got out of the car and waved at them, then went around front and collected her things from the passenger's seat. When she made it to the porch and asked if the two of them had been outside all day, Ash lied and told Mummy "No" and crossed her fingers behind her back—hoping against hope that her mother would fall for it.

"Is Daddy inside?" she asked, and Ashley nodded.

"But he's sleeping," Ash told her. "We didn't want to wake him up. So we thought we'd come out and play a bit more."

Mummy nodded, then Ashley and Michael followed her inside. When she said "Hello," Daddy mumbled something that sounded like "Oh spit!" and Ash could hear him shuffling around in a panic from the other room. But then he was quiet for a moment. By the time he came to the open door that divided living room from dining room, he was all smiles. He ruffled Michael's hair and smiled down at him—as if *Michael* was the one who had rescued him, and not Ashley—then he apologized for nodding off, for not getting dinner started.

Ash crossed her fingers again, this time so that they wouldn't fight. And they didn't. So they all went on with their day, kids and parents both, like nothing had happened at all.

They all went on with their lives.

LIVES THAT LED US HERE, Ashley thought to herself as she sat in the airport that day, waiting for her flight home to Boston. *Lives that led me to...*

But maybe he'd fallen asleep before her first scene. That was the thought Ashley clung to, as she tried *not* to think about what Ada had said about consequences—as she tried *not* to admit that maybe, for once, the old witch was right.

7

T he hardest thing about going back to work after all that had happened—the hardest of *many* hard things—was knowing the customers' stories before they told them. Ashley had always taken a certain amount of pride in her powers of deduction and observation—her ability to turn to a coworker and predict what the deal was with some guy who'd just walked in the door—but now it felt like she was cheating. She didn't even have time to guess before she just *knew*.

It took all the fun out of things. And without the fun, what was the point?

❦

W HEN HE WALKED into the club that night, Bones was gacked out of his mind with exhaustion. Which was better, he realized, than all the years he'd spent gacked out of his mind on coke and crank, but still not good. He'd been driving without sleep for more hours than he could count, through at least one sunrise and two sunsets. So, when he took a seat at the side of the runway and the waitress told him it was a two-drink minimum, he ordered two black coffees instead of a couple pints of the cheapest swill they had on tap.

Which was good, Ashley wanted to tell him, because this place didn't have any swill to speak of; they'd lost their liquor license years ago, years before Ash had even started dancing there. But she couldn't tell him, because they hadn't met yet; she was still backstage, waiting for her set to begin.

When Bones took his coffees from the waitress, he asked about getting a beer later if he was up for it. And that's when she told him what was what.

At first he was disappointed—that's what he'd tell Ashley in a little while, when they finally met and started shooting the shit—but then the other part of what the waitress told him finally hit home, the words repeating in his mostly numb skull: *full nude*.

Because there was no liquor in here, the ladies could—to borrow a phrase from the warrior poet Kesha—dance until their pants came off. Their panties, too. In here, the performers could get buck-ass nekkid and no one would get in trouble. This made tired old Bones smile. In twenty minutes time, once he was awake enough to enjoy it, he'd be over in the alcove, between the two ferns, with a totally naked chick in his lap, her pussy grinding against his thigh through jeans he hadn't washed in weeks. And she'd have a look on her face that convinced him that she liked it. Which—*who knows?*—she might. It took all kinds, right?

Ashley wondered, as she waited for her turn on stage, if she *would* like it—if that kind of dirtiness might do it for her tonight, that kind of pushing the envelope. But then the DJ called her to the stage and the time for thinking was done.

Dancing had become her one, final refuge from the knowledge her newfound powers cursed her with. Not the private dances, mind you—she was too close to the other person to shut things off then—but when she was up on stage, that's when she could move fast enough to outrun the thoughts that chased her.

But whether it was because the crowd was sparser that night, or because the rest of the night was going to be way more important than any of the nights before, Ashley couldn't dodge things the way she'd gotten used to. She just kept seeing Bones, kept seeing what he was thinking.

When the DJ called Ashley to the stage, Bones—still half out of it—swore that the pole she was swinging around was not a pole at all. What he saw there, sprouting up from the lacquered floor and stretching up to the ceiling, was the dogwood tree growing in his parents yard back home—the one his elementary school sent home with him on Arbor Day twenty some-odd years before.

He had always wanted to make love with someone beneath that tree. Beneath *any* tree, for that matter. With a pond nearby— that would've been nice, too. Some leaves on the ground, like the pair of orange panties that Ashley had just pushed off of herself and onto the stage floor. *Some leaves*, thought Bones, *but not many*. What he longed for was the beginning of autumn, not the end.

And maybe, he thought, this would be with a smaller woman, like the woman—Ashley—who had just slapped her ass in exchange for the dollar bill he'd offered her. *Yes*, he thought, maybe a woman as slight in form as he was slight in soul. He'd only ever been with bigger girls, and he wondered what it would be like to be with someone as fragile as he was. Someone who understood how easy it was to break someone, someone who might treat him more gently than those who had come before.

But the one thing he was looking for above all else in this fantasy of his, the key word in all of it, was the word 'with.' He wanted to make love *with* someone, not *to*.

The first time he read it put that was was in a short story, something he read in college by a guy from the 70s and from the south. Bones didn't know if *with* was just something they said down there, or back then, but he liked it. He liked how one word could make all the difference in the world.

Ashley liked it, too. She would have to remember to tell him so when he told her this story.

In his mind's eye, as Ashley danced, Bones was under the tree, with a woman who was just as sick of having things done *to* her as he was sick of doing things *to* someone. As sick as he was of someone who didn't seem interested, who just laid there and waited for it to be over.

He set another dollar bill on the rail and waited for Ashley to come and collect it. And he tried to collect himself as he waited, tried to collect a string of words he might offer her when she arrived.

But it was Ashley who spoke first.

"Would you like a dance," she asked him, "after I'm done?"

She'd crouched down to pose her question. Her naked chest was right there in front of him, her crotch too, but he stared right into her eyes instead.

Ashley arched an eyebrow and asked him if that was a yes.

Under the tree with *her*, he imagined. *With* her. On a blanket, the two of them laughing together as dead leaves tumbled into living places. The two of them making something with each other. *With*.

"Yes," said Bones. "Abso-fucking-lutely. I would fucking love to dance with you, honey."

"With?" said Ashley.

"Yes," he said. "With, with, with."

⚜

ASHLEY SAT with Bones for a while after the dance, in part because he'd tipped so well and in part because she was afraid for the guy. His rig was parked across the street in the huge parking lot of the mall, and he had a bed in the cab where he could conk out until morning, but it sounded to Ashley like he was going to press on as soon as he left the club. And that didn't seem like a good idea at all. So she decided to tucker him out instead, with a bit of mindless conversation.

"Why 'Bones'?" she asked, figuring there must be a story behind the nickname. But of course, before he could even get started with his explanation, she knew what he was going to say. His last name was McCoy, and he loved him some *Star Trek*.

When he finished the story, he asked her if she'd ever watched the show.

"I watched *Next Gen*," she said. "Bit of *Deep Space Nine*."

Bones nodded. "Those are on my bucket list," he said. "I mean to get to 'em before I'm gone. Just haven't found the time."

Ashley smiled at the notion of someone actually having a bucket list. She knew it was a thing people *talked* about making, but she'd never met someone who'd actually done it.

"It's saved my life more'n a few times," he said.

"The list?" asked Ashley.

Bones nodded again. "Yep," he said. "Keeps me from doing anything too stupid."

Ashley smiled. "And what happens when you cross everything off?" she asked.

But instead of answering her, Bones inched forward in his seat just enough that he could dig into his back pocket for his wallet. Once he had it in hand, he settled back into his seat and began to search through the wallet for his list. And it wasn't long before he'd pulled it forth and handed it over.

Ashley unfolded it and was flabbergasted. It looked like it had been torn from a notebook an age and a half ago, the paper worn thin at the creases. And he'd covered the damn thing, front and back, with his too-tiny, nigh-indecipherable scrawl. Only about half of the items on the front page had been crossed off, but that hadn't stopped him from coming up with new ideas. He'd begun to fill in the margins, now that he'd run out of space everywhere else.

"You ever tried making one yourself?" Bones was about to ask her, and she fought hard not to reply before he got the question out of his mouth.

"No," she said, once he'd spoken. "I haven't."

જ્ઞુજી

AND MAYBE *THAT* was what she needed: a bucket list, a bunch of things to do to keep her distracted. It was anyone's guess how long it would take until she ended up frail in the 40s, with that soldier boy who seemed nice enough but was no Robin Gates. So why not find something to do in the meantime?

The moment Ashley was home for the night, passing Mum asleep on the couch and Dad asleep in front of his computer, she grabbed the notebook and pen out of her duffle and got to work.

But sitting there on her bed, curled up under the covers, she ran into a problem: after nearly every item she wrote down, that aggravating voice in the back of her head uttered its favorite word to her: "*Nope*."

She tried to push past it, to keep pen on paper until she was done. That was the secret to writing anything, after all—at least according to her cousin Matt, the author of the family. But eventually the *nopes* were too many and too persistent, like a thousand Agent Smiths piling on top of Neo in *The Matrix*. Eventually, Ashley had to throw in the towel—which she did, of course, by throwing the pen and paper across the room and into the wall.

Ashley closed her eyes and did her best to clear her head, and for the first time since her return home, it actually worked. She felt empty inside, hollow—a vessel waiting to be filled. But rather than fill herself up again with thoughts—and thoughts *about* thoughts—she was able to sit still for a good second or two with nothing on her mind at all.

Until the pleasant feeling of having nothing on her mind *became* the thing on her mind.

She opened her eyes and threw off the covers. Then she crossed the room to collect her notebook.

As she sat again, Ashley reviewed what she'd written. And she sighed as she looked down the list, nearly everything on it too aspirational by far. She'd been focusing too much on what *other* people might do if they knew they only had so much time left.

What *Robin* would have done, she realized.

But Robin had her chance, Ashley said to herself. And that was true. Robin had *years* of knowing that her time was running out. And if she didn't do enough with that knowledge, that was *her* problem.

Did Robin not do enough? Is that what Ashley was saying? She shuddered at the thought, the *accusation*. Then she teared up at it.

Without thinking about it, Ashley wrote *Kiss Robin again* on the list. And while she fully expected the voice in her head to utter its "*Nope*" once again, the voice said nothing.

"Seriously?" she said aloud, but there was no reply. And that silence was the sweetest sound she'd heard in a good, long while.

So she kept writing, chasing that absence of noise until the sun was rising outside her bedroom window. Then she chased it some more.

8

One evening, the club played host to a crowd of Christian kids who'd congregated there to pass judgement—their favorite pastime. And though Ashley did her best to avoid looking at them and their exhausting glares of disapproval, all it took was one overlong glance in their general direction for their story to begin playing out in her head.

Once God was done sculpting her, they were saying, she must've taken to sculpting herself. And once she'd done all that she could do on her own, she'd opened her purse to someone who could sculpt her even further.

"Or her legs," said the one girl at their table. She glared at the stage, at Ashley, then took a deep pull from her glass of Diet Coke.

They said these things with rolls of their eyes, or with knowing nods, looking for Danny to nod along with them or to grunt his assent. But he didn't.

Danny, Ashley realized, was the one she'd spend time with. The rest didn't matter, thank god.

When Danny argued to his friends that Ashley might just

have a fast metabolism, they swore that was nothing but code for anorexia or bulimia.

"It's not," Danny told them, "but even if it were, those problems are nothing to laugh at."

But they did laugh. They laughed at him. They laughed at the girls working the tables and soliciting private dances. "There's loving your neighbor," they told Danny. "And there's loving *sinners*."

When he persisted, when he tried to tell them that he knew what he was talking about—when he tried to tell them about how his sister almost died the summer she turned thirteen, they rolled their eyes at him.

The girl at the table scoffed. "You just want to fuck her," she said.

A couple of the others looked affronted by the girl's language. One even put his hand on her arm to ask if she was okay, but she just shrugged him off. Then she held up her hand to signal a waitress and ordered another Diet Coke.

Which she didn't tip for, of course.

Danny turned his back on his friends then and turned his attention to the stage instead. Ashley was collecting her clothes from the catwalk now, and Danny was trying to remember her name, what the DJ said her name was. And he felt ashamed that he couldn't.

But then he felt ashamed at his shame, because he was watching her and she wasn't like any of the other girls he'd seen up there before. She collected her clothes and balled them up in her hand, not using them to cover herself up as she headed offstage. She seemed proud of her body, maybe even prouder of it when it was naked then when it was hidden beneath clothes.

And why shouldn't she be? Danny wondered. Her body was God's gift to her, wasn't it? Why shouldn't she embrace it, be thankful for it?

You just want to fuck her. The words repeated in his head, a record skipping.

Yes, of course, because why else might he try to defend her? What other reason might there be? Humanity wasn't a thing anyone believed in anymore. And empathy? That was dead, too.

"You can't save someone who won't save themself"—that's what Danny's friends were saying now. And empathy? They were *so* over that shit.

But Danny wasn't, not yet, which was why he got up from the table and made a bee-line for Ashley. And it wasn't until he saw someone flinch in the shadows—the bouncer, he realized almost too late—that he slowed himself down.

She couldn't have been dressed for more than thirty seconds when he asked her for a dance.

"Sure," said Ashley. "But this song is shit. You mind if we wait for the next one?"

Danny nodded, she nodded back, and then Ashley took his hand, walking him over to an alcove surrounded by tall ferns. There were four couches there—two against the wall and another two facing the first pair—with enough space for eight people. *Just* enough, Danny realized, as Ashley wove them through three dances already underway. When they took seats on the only couch that was still free, Danny sat to one side. Ashley leaned back into the cushioned arm on the other, then draped her legs over his lap.

"You don't mind," she said, "do you?"

Danny shook his head.

"Legs are sore," she said. "Been a long night."

And before he knew what he was doing, he was massaging her calves. "Oh," he said, stopping for a second as he realized, "am I allowed—?"

She smiled at him. "Dude," she said, "I wouldn't put my legs there if you weren't allowed. I'm not an asshole."

Danny laughed.

"Just stick to the calves," she said. "If you move to my shins, you're going to find that spot I missed shaving this morning. And we don't want to ruin the illusion now, do we?"

He laughed again. But then the song ended, and he fell silent. And Danny realized that, while part of this might very well be an illusion, part of it was very, very real. And that part—*that* part—he had no idea what to do with.

He looked around the alcove and watched as two of the other dances stopped altogether. The third paused for a second, just long enough for some negotiation to be made, and then continued. Danny gulped, ashamed. Ashamed and not sure where to look. Was it any better to watch one of the two women getting dressed now than it was to watch the one woman who was still writhing on some old man's lap? Or was it actually worse? He didn't know, so he didn't choose. He didn't look at any of them. He looked down instead.

But now he was looking at a pair of legs resting on his lap. And now a new song was starting. And now he had *no idea* what was going to happen. He thought of the friends he came with, and whether they could even *be* friends after this. Whether they would ever speak to him again. Then he tried to think of why he came to this woman in the first place, of what he wanted to happen, what he wanted to say. And how quickly she took control. Maybe she *did* have a bit of the devil in her. And maybe *this* was his temptation. Maybe this strip club was his desert and God was testing him *right now*. And maybe—

"Another clunker," said Ashley with a groan. "We'll wait one more."

"Okay," he said. And he sighed.

"You can look at me," she said, as if reading his mind. "You have my permission." And then, when still he didn't look at her, she added, "I'm not naked yet."

Danny looked up and looked at Ashley. And he saw something close up that he hadn't seen from across the room. It was in her eyes and her lips. In the photo of her out in the tiny lobby, where the bouncer had checked their IDs, it was almost as if she—or her photographer—had calculated just how open her eyes should be, and how big she could smile before she stopped looking "hot" and started looking genuine. Now, looking at Danny, it was like she couldn't care less what she looked like. She smiled so big that her eyes looked like they were being squished between her cheeks and her eyebrows. It was a smile so big that it was almost a laugh. And it was cute. Cute, not hot.

But she didn't care, Danny saw. And that amazed him.

"So," she said, "your friends seem like fun."

He laughed.

"Are they gonna ditch you?" she asked.

Danny wasn't sure, and that's what he told her.

"And what made you come over?" she asked. "What made you stop judging? The thing about glass houses?"

"What?" he asked.

"Isn't there some Bible verse about glass houses, or something?"

"There's something in Matthew," he said, "about specks and logs—"

"Logs?" she said, her eyebrow arched like a question mark.

He sighed. "It wasn't because of a Bible verse anyway," he said. "I came over because of my name."

"Huh?" she said.

"God is my judge," he said. "That's what my name means."

"Oh," she said, and she still looked confused. "What's your name?"

"Damn," he said, shaking his head. "I forgot. I, uh, I'm Danny."

"Danny," she said, nodding. "Suits you."

"That's what Mom and Dad were hoping for," he said. "I suppose."

"Not judgy people?" she asked.

"No," he said, shaking his head. "They were the judged."

"Oh," she said, "but sometimes the judged are the judgiest."

Another song ended, but still she did not move her legs. Danny did some math in his head, suddenly unsure if he was being charged for each of the songs they'd skipped. "I'm not sure I can—"

"Not sure about what?" she asked.

"Do I owe you for each of these songs?" he asked, reaching under her legs and into his pocket.

"Nah, man," she said. "We're just chatting."

"Okay," he said, and he sighed in relief.

"Besides," she said, "I'm not sure you're up for it."

"What?" he said. "Not up for what?"

"A dance," she said.

"Well," he said, stuttering, "I wouldn't, uh... I wouldn't have asked if—"

"If you weren't a knight in shining armor," she said, and she gave him a twisted grin like she'd figured him out and she was waiting for him to tell her she was wrong.

But Danny realized, quite suddenly, that she wasn't. Wrong, that is.

"Don't feel bad," she said. "I've been working here since I was 18. I've sat on the lap of just about every kind of guy there is."

He wanted to get up now, but she wasn't moving her legs. He shuffled in his seat to make his intentions known, but she was stronger than he was. He noticed, only then, how muscled her legs were. They weren't huge, the muscles, but they were there. And she knew how to use them.

"Hold up," she said. "I know you want to get out of here now, but hold up a second. Okay?"

Danny inhaled. Deep. Then he settled himself back into the seat and he nodded.

"I'll give you the dance of your life," she started to say, but he cut her off.

"I don't want," he started to say, but then *she* cut *him* off.

"Yes," she said. "Yes, you do." And to prove her point, she flexed a calf just enough for him to notice that he was, in fact, hard as a rock.

"But," she said, "I don't think you're ready for what happens at the end of it. When you're walking back to your table, wondering if the cum stain is going to be obvious through your jeans, when you realize that you can't rescue me—"

"I don't want to—"

She held two fingers to his lips to shush him. "When you realize I don't want to be rescued," she said, "how are you going to handle that?"

"My sister," he blurted out, and he realized that was probably the most awkward thing he could've said in there, in that position. But she didn't flinch, so he continued. He clarified. "She's why I really came over. She—"

"She's hot?" Ashley asked him.

"No," he said. "Or, well, maybe. I don't know. She's my sister."

She smirked at him, though this smirk was kinder than the last one.

"She almost died when she was thirteen."

"Shit," said Ashley. "What happened?"

He told the story, trying at first to invent a version fit for the venue, then abandoning all pretense.

"That's horrible," said Ashley.

"And so," he said, "when my friends started in on how skinny you are—"

She laughed. "I'm not *that* skinny." She laughed again. "Jesus, if they think *I'm* skinny..."

"So," he said, "I guess that's why I came over. I want to show that, um, that..." But then he trailed off, because he wasn't sure what he wanted to show. He wasn't sure what he was trying to prove.

Another song ended. This time, though, Ashley got up. "I like

89

this song," she said, and she started to fiddle with the zipper on her top. "You ready?" she asked.

"Ready for what?" he said, because he really didn't know what she wanted him to do now. What she wanted him to *say*.

"You tell me," she said.

He stood and reached into his pocket for his wallet, but she took gentle hold of his arm and stopped him.

"Save it," she said. "For your therapist, or the collection plate."

"I—" he started to say, but she shushed him again.

And then—with her two fingers pressed to his lips, with him breathing in the scent of the private places she'd rubbed with those fingers when she was up on stage, the dark places he suddenly wished he were brave enough to explore—then she said, "Or save it for when you're ready." She gave him a fierce look, made a promise with her eyes, and she said, "I'll be here."

9

It was her first time in a courthouse, and Ashley knew the moment she stepped into the elevator that morning that it would also be her last. That was a comfort at least. If only the same could be said for the guy she was stuck with inside that cramped lift, a guy so full of conflict that it made Ashley's head quake to be this close to him.

He was a Robert on his business card, but a Bobby to anyone who asked. Robert Jackson, attorney at law. Not her lawyer, but *a* lawyer, and that made this Bobby an observant fellow. A studious man. And what he was studying right now was Ashley's ass.

And feeling bad about it, of course. The guilt in the elevator that day was so thick you could slice it and serve it at a Church picnic. And it was this that made Ashley queasy: not the fact of knowing what he was doing, but having to feel the feelings he was feeling about doing it.

These powers of hers were getting to be more of a pain in the ass every day.

Bobby had been staring for five minutes, staring at her booty as intently as she was staring at the unmoving indicator of their stalled elevator. But Bobby had yet to figure out what it was that

Ashley had stuffed into her back pocket. That seemed to be what was vexing him now. He'd considered many options while checking her out, even wondering for a moment if the tight slacks had been painted on (like they were doing in the *Swimsuit Issue* now), but it was the unsightly bulge that kept capturing his attention.

When Ashley pulled a lighter from the pocket—a blue plastic one, like his mama used to use—Bobby was crestfallen. The derriere that a moment before looked poured into her pants like sand from her perfect hourglass—it looked uncomfortable now, like too much of her had been crammed into too little space. Bobby had ached for her, but now he *ached* for her, wondering what she'd put herself through to look like this. He wondered suddenly if, like his mother, cigarettes were a trick of her trade.

But he didn't say a word to her until she started to fiddle with the lighter and bring flame forth from it. It was only then, when she violated some law he didn't even realize he'd passed through both houses of the legislature in his head—it was only then that he spoke.

"You can't do that in here," he said

Ashley wheeled around, pretending to be startled, as if she hadn't realized until that very moment that someone was in there with her.

"It's unsafe," said Bobby.

"A stuck elevator is unsafe," is what she said in reply, before stepping back against the closed doors.

"You shouldn't lean against those," he said.

She quit her leaning but didn't move any closer to him than she had to. Then she got back to fiddling with her lighter, flicking the flame on and off.

With his eyes still locked on the flame, Bobby asked, "What brings you to the courthouse?"

She laughed. "Few months back, this guy comes into the club where I work. We have a nice enough time together, till he can't afford a second dance with me. So, he leaves with blue balls because I won't give him a freebie."

"That," he said, "is not a crime."

"I know," said Ashley. "But doing 60 in a 35 *is*."

"I don't follow."

"The guy," said Ashley, "the one who came into the club—it turns out he's a cop. And I guess those balls must be cerulean by now, because listen: he pulled me over, and I swear he was about to let me off with a warning. *Buuuuttt*, once he realized who I was... Man, you've never seen a warning turn into a ticket that fast."

They stood in silence for a few minutes then, stood there exhaling awkwardness and inhaling tension until Ashley caught Bobby staring again. Whether he was staring at her or just into the middle distance, she couldn't be sure. But she figured a playful jab couldn't hurt, and would at least keep them from suffocating under the pressure of an air thick with unease.

"You're staring."

He looked up at her face and shook his head. He'd been lost in his own brain for a spell, but he wondered if it *looked* like he was staring. That would be just as incriminating. Looking for a way out, he nodded at her hand and the lighter she'd clutched there. A misdirect. His specialty.

"The lighter?" she said.

"The lighter," he said.

"Not my tits?" she asked, feigning disappointment.

"No," he said.

"It's bothering you *that* much?"

Bobby nodded again.

She held her hands up like a cop show criminal who's trying not to get shot, as if a white woman looking the way she did would *ever*. Get shot, that is. For *anything*. As if she'd ever face more than a slap on the wrist for her transgressions.

As Ashley heard that thought of his, the fact of Bobby's blackness struck her for the first time. So she stuffed the lighter back into her pocket and decided to give the guy a break.

"First offense?" he asked her.

Ashley gave him a curt laugh, then asked, "First elevator?"

"Oh no," said Bobby, "I'm a connoisseur."

"A connoisseur?" she said. "Of elevators?"

"Yes, ma'am."

And it was true. When he was a boy, he often did that little kid thing where he would not walk the rest of the mall—absolutely would *not*—until his mother let him ride the elevator.

It was innocent at first, just a kid pushing boundaries and enjoying the closest thing to a ride he'd get outside of Mama's company trip to Canobie Lake Park. But then he started to study the inspection certificates, and the ways the numbers were shaped on the buttons, and whether the numbers lit up or not. Bobby noted which lifts had windows, which ones played music, and whether they ever played anything good. In high rises in the city where he went to law school, he always looked for a thirteenth floor. Just in case. And if he found one, which he did a couple of times, he got out and took the stairs. Bobby didn't believe in much besides the law, but he did believe in bad luck.

He realized now, after a lifetime spent with his face hidden in books—and a childhood spent hiding behind his mother's skirts before that—he realized what he must've looked like those couple times he took a detour to avoid the thirteenth floor. Who the fuck did that? The people he passed as he came back in through the door marked Emergency Exit—those suited-up white folks—what must they have thought of him and his thrift store suit? A black man in the stairwell? Well, *shit*. That man *must* be up to no good.

"In all your years of riding elevators," Ashley was asking him now, "you've never once seen someone play with a lighter to pass the time?"

"Well, it's not," he said, "strictly speaking, legal."

She rolled her eyes at him. "And I suppose," she said, "you like to do things by the books."

"Comes with the territory," he said, gesturing with his hands to the elevator doors and the courthouse beyond.

Ashley shook her head and returned her attention to the still unmoving indicator. They passed another minute in silence, Bobby's eyes focused on the floor now, on the cracks in the tile there. Then, finally, Ash spoke.

"Were you checking out my ass?"

"No, ma'am," he said.

"Because, strictly speaking, that wouldn't be polite."

"Strictly speaking," he said.

"But before," she said, "when I had my back to you the last time?"

"You are not," said Bobby, "the center of my attention. No, ma'am."

"I *am* the most interesting thing in this elevator."

Bobby scoffed. "You forget," he said. "I'm a connoisseur."

"Of asses too, I'll bet."

He threw his head up to stare at her and found that she was smiling down at him.

"I mean," she said, "it's right at eye level, after all."

"I'm not that—"

"Don't front," she said. "Own it, dude. I mean, for real: men of your stature are in short supply."

"Shrek?!" he said, the spit that flew from his mouth one part venom and two parts incredulity. "Girl, did you just Shrek me?"

"Ain't no shame in being a little dude," she said. "Remember Kid Rock's sidekick? What was his name?"

"Joe C," he said, not sure if this conversation could get any worse.

"Yes," she said. "Joe C. That's him."

"And what about him?" asked Bobby.

"Well," she said, "if the song's to be believed, he mighta been three foot nine—"

"I *ain't* three foot nine."

"But," she said, "he had a ten foot dick."

"Are you asking me how big my penis is?"

"Nope," she said, shaking her head. "I'd rather keep imagining it."

Bobby blushed now, and sighed, realizing—*finally!*—that she was fucking with him. But he knew his shit wasn't big, and something in him felt obligated to correct her assumption. After all, a seemingly positive stereotype is still a stereotype. And so, he started to say "Just so you know, despite rumors to the contrary, not all black men—"

But she cut him off before he could finish. "You know," she said, holding a hand above his head and then pulling it towards herself—and slanting downward near the end for effect—"you are *actually* just the right height."

"Girl," he said, blushing even more now, "don't play. It was funny before, but we both know I ain't getting it."

She laughed. "You could," she said. "Get it, I mean."

"Bullshit," he said.

"You hear about that show," she said, "the one they're making for HBO? With all the swords and the sex?"

"*Game of Thrones?*" he asked, though what else could she be talking about?

"Yes!" she said. "The short guy they just cast in that—"

"Peter Dinklage," he added.

"Yes," she said. "Him. I hear that, in the books at least, he gets *all* the pussy."

"Well yeah," he said. "But he's Peter Dinklage. He's a god among dwarfs."

And now *she* sighed. "Why do so many guys find it so hard to imagined that I'd fuck them if given the chance?"

Bobby punched the button for the third floor once and then

again. "I don't want your pity," he said. But he took another look at her as he said it, and suddenly he wasn't so sure of his resolve. When pity looked like that, how could one refuse it?

"Fuck you," she said, pushing the button herself. "I don't *do* pity."

And now she moved behind him, so that he couldn't stare, to make sure that he wouldn't.

It was only a few moments later that he heard her playing with the lighter again.

He sighed. Then Bobby stared at the number that would not move, at the countdown he prayed would begin now. Or now. Or in just a second.

And though she didn't do it out loud, Ashley prayed with him.

10

On any other day, Ashley wouldn't have worn socks. She would have showered and spent extra time washing her feet, cleaning between her toes, so that all that was left to smell when the kid slipped off her boots was the scent of soft leather.

On any other day, she would have kept her eyes open to watch him bury his nose in the arch of her foot. She would have kept her eyes open to watch him close his own, to see him rub his nose along the length of her sole. Back and forth, until she giggled, until she said "Stop!" through peals of breathless laughter.

But this wasn't any other day. It was today, and her foot was dirty as fuck. So her eyes were closed, and she felt the closest to shame she had in years.

❧

THEY MET IN THE CLUB, on a night when he and his friends from college lined the catwalk on both sides. One of them had just transitioned, and they were taking him out to celebrate—to welcome him to "the world of men," a phrase they couldn't say without laughing derisively.

"The world of men is over," one of them growled, in a shitty approximation of an orc from *The Lord of the Rings*. Shitty, yes, but they all laughed anyway—and Ashley almost joined in. But she was still on stage, and as laid back as she got when she worked the floor, the stage was still a stage. And she had the rest of her set to get through before she let them see the girl behind the curtain.

They were all hopelessly awkward, putting fives on the tip rail because they were worried about looking cheap. They had just read an essay in English Comp which argued for the fair treatment of sex workers. But for one of them, the guy who'd just transitioned, this field trip wasn't purely academic. He was too shy to say it out loud, so he said it in the way that he looked at Ashley.

When Ash was done with her set on stage, she crouched to consult with the leader of the pack. "Your friend," Ash said, "would he be okay with a dance?"

"Okay?"

"I don't want to fuck him up," she said. "I imagine it's a sensitive time. But he looks like he could use it. And I *think* he wants it, but I don't want to be wrong." She paused and threw a smile at the guy they were talking about. "This time especially, I don't want to be wrong."

"Shit," he said, a big fucking grin on his face, "I think she'd—"

The pronoun stopped him dead in his tracks, and Ashley could see in the set of his jaw that he was gritting his teeth. "Fuck," he said. "He," he said. "He, he, *he*."

Ashley slapped his knee. "Stop it," she said. "You misgender him once, it's not the end of the world."

"No," he said. "There's no excuse, no fucking—"

Ashley lifted his chin, made him look at her. "No," she said. "There is no excuse. You gotta get that shit right. But don't make a big deal of it every time you get it wrong. Don't make it about *you*."

"Right," he said, nodding.

"So," she said, "you want to keep working on it while I give him a dance?"

He patted his pants pockets, one then the other, and frowned. "I think I'm out," he said.

She stood and she ruffled his hair. "You guys put enough up on that rail tonight that I think I can spot you."

Then she sauntered over to the friend and held out her hand to be kissed like she was Kate fucking Winslet in *Titanic*. "Sir," she said.

He smiled at her and played along, taking her hand in his own and bringing it to his lips.

"I know this is forward," said Ashley, "but I'm wondering if you'd ask me for—"

"A dance?" he said.

"Yes," she said, and she squeezed his hand ever so slightly to get him to stand up.

He did stand, and he brushed his hands across the front of his jeans—as if they weren't immaculate already. Then he shoved his hands into his pockets and shifted awkwardly from one foot to the other.

"Sir," said Ashley, pouting a little, "aren't you going to offer me your arm?"

He smiled, offered his arm, and then stood still for a second as Ashley took it. "Where do we go?" he asked out of the corner of his mouth.

Ashley nodded in the direction of the fern-shrouded alcove and they were underway.

"I'm nervous," he told her. "I've never done anything like this before."

"Never danced?" she said, playing coy, but overdoing it on purpose.

He laughed, and he relaxed.

Once Ashley had him seated, once she'd nudged his legs open

until he was full-on man-spreading, she leaned over and asked him if there was anything off-limits.

He chuckled. "I thought I was supposed to ask you that."

"It's your dance," said Ashley.

He inhaled, long and deep. Then he said "No. No boundaries."

WHEN THEY WERE DONE and he was breathless, Ashley led Jay back to his friends. Jay—that was his name, and he seemed almost more turned on by Ashley breathing his name into his ear than he was by any grind or bounce.

Jay's friends were too quiet, so Ashley squeezed Jay's hand and stopped short of the table the friends had all moved to while Jay was away.

"Excuse me," said Ashley. When they still looked confused, she held her free hand to the back of one ear lobe and pushed it toward them ever so slightly.

"What?" said the leader of the pack.

"Make some fucking noise!" said Ashley.

They clapped, but not loud enough for her. So she rolled her eyes and turned to face Jay again, to see if he was up for what she had in mind. She asked the question with her eyes and waited. When she was sure the answer was yes, she pulled Jay close and kissed him full on the lips. Jay's tongue pushed Ashley's lips open like it had a mind of its own, or at least like it was his brain's official translator.

And now, finally, the friends hollered. They whistled.

Ashley broke the kiss slowly, holding Jay's face in her hands until it was just a little less flushed, until he'd caught his breath.

Then, as her goodbye, she turned around and shook her ass against Jay's crotch one last time.

WHEN SHE SAW the leader of the pack again, it was in the window of a Starbucks in Cambridge. She was with another girl from the club, walking back from Hubba Hubba to the Harvard T station—their arms laden with bags and bags of fetish gear—when the other girl said "Isn't that the guy from the other night?"

"Jay?" said Ashley, squinting to see if she could spot him through the window.

"Nah," said Nikki. "The other one. The hottie."

Ashley frowned at Nikki. "Jay was hot," she said.

"Yes," said Nikki. She sighed. "I didn't mean anything by it. Just because I'm older than you doesn't mean I'm any less open-minded."

Ashley rolled her eyes. Nikki wasn't a bad person, not overall, but she *had* looked a little uncomfortable when Ash told her the full story of that night. She'd fucking *winced* once, so Ashley thought it was fair she let Nikki know she still had work to do.

Now that she knew who she was looking for, Ashley pressed her face to the window again. She spotted him almost immediately, and he spotted her. Their waves hello were pretty damn near synchronized.

Ashley and Nikki stood in line, ordered, and asked him when he got off. He smiled knowingly at their choice of words, and it was while they waited for their lattes that Nikki told Ashley the kid was definitely into her.

"Into me?" Ashley joked. "Not yet, but give me an hour."

AND NOW THEY were in his dorm room. A single, thank god. No roommate to interrupt them, though Ashley knew she'd have to keep it down once they got to business. Last thing she wanted was to have to explain to some R.A. why she was fucking a kid ten years younger than she was.

A kid who was telling her to keep her eyes closed and to stop laughing.

"Okay," she said, "but you gotta get away from my foot. It's nasty."

But now he was using his tongue on it, the filthy thing. He was licking her foot—licking. her. *foot*—and in a way that wasn't at all funny. In a way that was actually, weirdly—very fucking weirdly —*hot*. Her breath caught in her throat as he made his way toward her big toe.

"Do you really want—?" she began to ask, but he'd pulled it into his mouth before she could finish the sentence.

Ashley realized this was probably the weirdest thing she had *ever* had done to her.

And yet.

Ashley opened her eyes and looked down at him. She was sitting on the edge of his desk, and he was kneeling on his floor. Sometime while she had her eyes closed, he'd managed to get his clothes off. And his dick was standing at full attention now, bobbing back and forth like a flag pole in a stiff breeze.

How *the fuck* was this turning him on? That was what Ashley wanted to know. But then she let that thought go. Because she could hear Nikki in her head, could see the delighted smirk on her friend's face as she asked "Who's closed-minded now?" And so, Ashley turned her attention from her foot to his cock.

She watched as it throbbed. And that—she reached down the front of her unbuttoned shorts to make sure—made her wet.

Holy shit, she thought. *Will you look at that?*

When it came right down to it, she realized—she *remembered* —the ultimate turn-on for her was to turn someone else on. Whatever it took.

And so, she moaned for him to "suck it." And when that stopped him for a moment, when the sound of her voice after so much silence stopped him in his tracks, she grabbed a fistful of his hair in each hand and put him back to work.

Soon there was more than one toe in his mouth. Soon, there was most of a foot. And pretty soon after that—he was a kid, after all, and still learning—she watched him spray the floor with his seed.

But that didn't stop him. If anything, it made him attack her foot even more eagerly than before. And fuck if his enthusiasm—and his facility with his tongue, and what she imagined he might do with it later—fuck if that didn't make her come, too.

☙❧

AT HOME THAT NIGHT, Ashley took out her bucket list and added that day's events to the sheet of paper. Then she crossed them out, and she smiled. She hadn't seen this day coming, and what a relief that was. What. A. Relief.

III

STAYIN' ALIVE

2011–2013

11

S he was the kind of girl who would never have acknowledged his existence, back in the day. But now, now that he was wrinkled and gray and round in the middle— now that he wasn't a threat, in other words, and not an option— now she not only acknowledged the fact of his being, but seemed also to relish the very notion of being in his presence. Now, Ashley sat on the other side of his desk and rambled absentmindedly about the race she planned to run the next year—as if she had nowhere better to be, as if his company was the best she could do on a Friday night.

The professor was a man who fixated on things. In the picture Ash dialed up on her phone from this past year's race, he couldn't stop staring at the splotches of blue paint on her tan thighs, the green paint spattered across her flushed face, the pink paint in her brown hair.

"People throw it at you," she explained, "as you run the race. To celebrate diversity."

"Must take forever to wash off," he said.

"Nah," she said, waving dismissively at him. "Besides," she said, "if it does take a bit longer than usual, isn't that the point?"

He smiled at her. She smiled back.

Then, finally, they turned to the subject of her paper: a personal narrative about her years as a stripper. He had just graded it. Too harshly, he thought, even with all of the tense changes and the spelling mistakes and the shifting points of view, given the effort she'd obviously put into it—but she didn't seem to disagree. No. Instead, she listened to his feedback and nodded—chewing on the eraser end of her pencil all the while. She wrote nothing down, but he didn't fault her for this. He wasn't really saying anything of interest anyway, nothing he hadn't already said more eloquently in writing. He was unfocused. Or, rather, he *was* focused, but on the wrong thing.

He was still thinking about paint-spattered thighs.

In her mind, hearing him thinking these things, Ashley felt the urge to grin. But she knew that even the slightest smile would make this more difficult for him than it already was, so she restrained the urge.

When he was through, she collected her bag and thanked him for his time. But on her way out the door, she paused, looked back over her shoulder, and finally gave him the smile she'd been holding back.

Back when he was a student himself and girls smiled at him like that, he wrote them love letters in return. He could've earned a PhD for his work on overreacting to simple kindnesses, the love-starved lad. They never spoke to him again after the letters, not any of them, but he didn't blame them. How could he? He may not have known it then, but he knew it now, staring at his reflection in his laptop's darkened screen.

He was a creep.

He was a creep, and he always would be. Good for them, he thought, for seeing that earlier than he did. Good for them for keeping a safe distance.

He slapped the lip of the laptop shut, then set his head down upon it. The aluminum wasn't as warm as he expected it to be. In fact, it was pleasantly cold. *The wonders of technology*, he thought. How *did* they get these things to run so cool nowadays? His first computer had been a veritable tank of plastic, its hard drives a pair of obnoxious spinning rims, its fans as loud as an aftermarket exhaust pipe—so loud it embarrassed him every time he opened it in public. The professor had never been one to make a show of things. Like the creep that he was, he had always been more comfortable lurking in the shadows. Unheard. Unseen.

There was a knock at the door. Startled out of the pits of his own despair, he snapped to attention.

"Yes?" he said.

Ashley was back and she was telling him not to stress about her grade. "I'm dropping out anyway," she said. When he asked her why, she told him that this was her second try at college, but that it wasn't sticking this time any better than it had the last.

"Well, I'm sorry to hear that," he told her. Then he offered her a weak smile.

"Not your fault," she said. "Your course is great. All of my courses are interesting, actually. But the whole enterprise, I still can't justify it. Cost/benefit analysis, you know?"

He nodded. "And the costs," he said, "are much higher these days." He was still nodding, he realized, and he felt self conscious about it, so he added "Too high" in the hopes of putting a full stop on the thought.

"But there are upsides," she said. "So don't be entirely glum."

"Upsides?" he said.

Ashley gave him a look then that he'd only seen a few times in his life. Or, well, it was a look that he'd only *noticed* a few times. And it wasn't until a colleague pointed it out to him in a bar, just after he'd missed what the colleague called "the most obvious opportunity of your life," that he'd had a name for it. The look, that is.

"Those were her Fuck-Me Eyes," the colleague had told him. And then she, the colleague, had given him a glance of her own to show him what she was talking about. He was hard in an instant, now that he knew what the look was meant to convey, and the colleague seemed to know it. So she excused herself and went to the bathroom to give him time to sort himself out.

That was the look that Ashley was giving him now as she said "The upside is that, in two weeks time, I won't be your student anymore."

Maybe, he realized, with a gulp so comically big that he might be a cartoon now—that he might be Pepé Le Pew to her Penelope Pussycat—maybe, just maybe, he wasn't such a creep after all.

Or maybe, whispered a voice in his head, *she just likes creeps*.

"A fortnight," she told him as she backed out of his office, and her use of that obscure word was just as arousing to him as the look in her eyes had been. "Grendel's," she said. "8 o'clock."

"And we'll see what happens?" he said.

"Whatever will be," she said with a smile, "will be."

๛

TWO WEEKS LATER, as she descended the stone steps of the bar and made her way underground, Ashley wondered how much she'd tell the professor—about why she'd given up, about why she'd come back to school in the first place, about what was next for her. And the voice inside herself answered, simply, *Everything*.

But once she and the prof were tucked into a corner by the fireplace, the green and yellow neon of a Cambridge Brewing Company sign glowing above them, he was filling every awkward silence with one anecdote or another—about the college, about this bar, or about the epic poem that gave this place its name.

"I've always found the sign a bit odd," said the professor with a chuckle. "The fearsome foe of Beowulf, the sinister scion of Cain, reduced to a cartoonish troll in a dunce cap."

"Is it a dunce cap?" Ashley asked. "I mean, those are pointy at the top, right? And he's balancing a cup of coffee on his head."

The professor smiled and nodded, conceding. "Well, whatever it is he's wearing, he seems rather grumpy about it."

"Could be he's mad about that enormous sandwich he's being made to carry," said Ashley. "Could be that, too."

"Or the salad bowl he's got in the other hand," said the professor.

"Or the inane babble of the customers he's serving," said Ashley, trying to continue the joke and realizing only too late what she'd just said. What she'd just implied.

The professor blushed and ducked his head.

Ashley reached a hand across the table, grabbed his hand, and gave it a squeeze.

He looked her in the eye once more, though far more sheepishly than before. Then he managed a quick smile before reaching for the pint of liquid courage he'd left mostly untouched since it had arrived.

Ashley looked around for the server, flagged them down, and asked for another round.

"You never did tell me what you plan to do next," said the professor, "now that you're calling it quits on school. Will you go back to working at the club?"

"Oh," said Ashley. "I never stopped. Sorry if I didn't make that clear in the paper."

"Oh," said the professor. "I didn't realize. The stories in your essay did feel rather past-tense to me."

"Well," said Ashley, "most things feel pretty past-tense to me these days."

"This date, for instance?" asked the professor, half-teasing and half-worried.

Ashley gave him a smirk in return for his bad joke. "Not what I meant," she clarified. "Just that I feel kinda like I'm going through the motions, like I've done all this before."

You have, said the voice in her head.

The professor nodded. "I hear that," he said, then he took

another long sip from his beer. "Like the song says 'every day is exactly the same.'"

Ashley perked up. "You know NIN?" she asked.

"I'm fifty," he said, "not dead."

"Used to love them," said Ashley. "These days, though, it's like every *song* is exactly the same."

The professor laughed. "That's how you know you're getting old," he said. "Just in case you weren't aware."

"Says the old pro," she replied, as she made room on the table for the server to set down their next round.

The professor raised his glass for a toast then, and Ashley followed suit. But then nobody said anything, and Ashley—more than a little buzzed at this point—couldn't restrain her laughter.

"We may be old," said the professor finally.

"One of us more so than the other," Ashley interjected, tilting her glass at him and spilling a bit of her drink in the process.

"But here's to never growing up," said the professor, feeling stupid even as he said it—not drunk enough yet to ignore the shame in spewing a cliché at a woman who had probably heard all the lines in the world at least twice by now.

"Cheers to that," said Ashley clinking her glass against his.

They each took a good long swallow, but it was Ashley who came up for air first. And as she set down her glass, she gave him the look—the look that meant it was time to finish up and get out of there.

❧

THAT NIGHT in the professor's bed, pleasantly exhausted from the exertions of a man who needed to get laid more often, Ashley dreamt of the woman she'd been dreaming of more and more with each passing week.

Ashley dreamt of herself, her older self, the self she'd seen with the soldier so long ago now—a *future* self who spoke in a voice Ashley that was only now realizing had been the voice inside her head all along. The voice behind the "nopes" and so much more.

They were sitting at a booth inside the Strumpet's Sister, Ashley and the woman she would become, and they were sitting in silence for the first time since these visits had begun. Ashley wanted to say something, but she knew better than to try. She knew that the words would not come, even if she opened her mouth. Her future self always spoke first. That was just the way things worked.

"I'm not going to bother you anymore," said the voice, once she was ready.

Ashley frowned. "It's never been a bother," she said. "Just a mystery," she said. "A puzzle I could never solve. When you were going to say something and when you weren't—I could never figure that out."

"The next part," said the voice, "the *last* part—that you have to navigate on your own."

"And what if I do things differently than you did?" asked Ashley.

"You won't," said the voice. "You *can't*."

"But what if I *do*?"

The voice looked across the booth's table at Ashley, and Ashley looked back. They each took a good, long look—at the woman Ashley would become, at the woman she had always been.

"In five months," began the voice, "at the end of April, you'll go to Hawaii."

"And?" said Ashley.

"You'll do what you did in Portland, right before all of this started."

"What did I do?" asked Ashley. "Fuck an escort? Scatter Robin's ashes into a river?"

The voice stood then and smiled down at Ashley. "You gave everything away."

E. CHRISTOPHER CLARK

"I'm going to Hawaii," said Ashley, "to give everything away?"

The voice nodded, stepping out of the booth. But she didn't go yet, didn't leave entirely. No, she lingered. There was something left to say, though she wasn't ready to say it yet. She was waiting. Waiting, for Ashley.

"To my brother?" said Ashley. "I'm going to give everything to my brother?"

"Nope," said the voice one last time, and she stepped backwards into the shadows at the edge of Ashley's dream. She melted into the darkness.

Ashley was going to shout out the name of her sister-in-law then, was going to ask if she was meant to give everything to Jenna instead—and then to ask what, exactly "everything" meant. But then she remembered someone else who was living in Hawaii now, someone who might need her help—who might need "everything" Ashley had to offer.

The kid who wasn't a kid anymore. Her niece. Tracy.

Ashley woke, crossed "hot for teacher" off her bucket list—the last thing she'd written down all those years before—and added something new.

12

It was the last day of Tracy's freshman year when Ashley touched down in Honolulu. She flirted with the registrar to find out where Trace's classroom was, then headed there straight away.

She could have gone right to her brother's house to crash—and probably should have, given the fact that she'd been on a plane for fourteen hours—but Ash wanted to see Tracy first. And she had no idea how much that would mean to her niece. It had been a rough year. A rough fucking year.

Tracy was in some bullshit Gen Ed class on cultural diversity, taught by a pasty-ass hag who was only slightly more woke than Rip Van Winkle. Lucky for Ashley: it was on the first floor. She tried knocking on the window, but the kid right there was passed out and surfing the waves of a weed dream. Then she tried knocking again. But though a few people heard her that time and tilted their heads in her general direction, Tracy wasn't one of them. And so, right after Ash knocked the third time, she tugged up on the hem of her crop top and flashed the whole lot of them.

It wasn't until Tracy's classmates started laughing that she looked up from the poem she was working on and saw her aunt's breasts pressed against the window.

"Does anyone know that woman?" the professor asked.

"*Person*," said Tracy, stuffing her shit into her backpack. "Don't assume."

⊛

As Tracy drove Ashley back to the house, she also managed to drive Ash crazy. She told Ashley she was bored and Ash asked her what the fuck she was talking about.

"Look at that," said Ashley, pointing toward the regal ridges of Diamond Head, which were downright luminous in the setting sun. "You're bored by *that*?"

"No," said Tracy. "I'm bored by a system that's teaching me the same way I'd be taught literally *anywhere* else. I came here," she said, "to be *here*."

"Then be here," Ashley told her. Then she held up a pack of butts and asked Trace if she minded.

Tracy shook her head no, and asked Ash to just roll down the window first. Then she continued. "It's not all on me," she said. "There's my professors, too."

"Professors," Ashley told her as she lit up, "are full of shit." She took her first drag, then added "My brother certainly is."

Tracy laughed. Because it was true. But then she thought of something. "What about that professor you hooked up with a couple months back?" she asked. "The cute one you told me about, with the dad bod?"

Ashley said nothing, but she did give Tracy a playful punch in the arm.

"The trick," said Ashley, "is to make them believe their shit don't stink. You do that and they'll let you get away with anything."

Tracy told her she didn't want to get away with anything, that she just wanted to learn.

"Then learn," Ashley told her. "You get on a prof's good side and they'll let you learn whatever you want. They assign a paper on..." Ash held a free hand out toward Tracy, looking for help. And when the kid didn't give it right away, she snapped her fingers.

"Kierkegaard?"

"Yes," said Ashley. "Whoever the fuck that is. They assign you a paper on the Queer Key Guard—"

"Kierkegaard," said Tracy, trying not to laugh. Trying and failing.

"Yes," said Ashley. She took another drag, a deep one, then exhaled. "They assign that, but you're like, 'Nah, bro, I want to write about...'"

She snapped her fingers again.

"Atheism in nineteenth century Denmark?" Tracy offered, blurting out the first thing that came to mind.

"Sure!" said Ashley, though Trace could see out of the corner of her eye that Ashley had no idea what she was talking about. Ash ashed her cigarette out the window and waited for clarification.

"Kierkegaard was Danish," Tracy explained. "And—"

"Doesn't matter to me," said Ashley, excited—*so* excited, in fact, that she flicked the rest of her butt out the window. Then she turned her body in the passenger seat to face her niece—even though Tracy had to keep giving her attention to the road. "But it doesn't matter that it doesn't matter to *me*," she said. "That's not the point. The point is that it matters to *you*."

Tracy had to admit: Ashley *was* onto something. Because the more Trace thought about it, the more that atheism in nineteenth century Denmark sounded like something that might just be worth investigating. But there was something else that was bugging Tracy about school, something deeper than boredom, and Ashley seemed to sense that.

"What else?" she asked, lighting up another cigarette. "What else is bugging you?"

"I might not even be back next year," said Tracy.

"Why?" asked Ashley in between drags.

"Money," said Tracy, and she sighed. "Mom and Des, they can't..." She sighed again. "The theater's taking a loss this season, a big one. And then there's the house. It's getting old, you know, and—"

"Well," said Ashley, "what about me?"

"What about you?" asked Tracy.

"Nobody has said shit about this to me," said Ashley. "And I've got *money*."

"Yeah," said Tracy, and her shoulders tensed as she thought about what Auntie Ashley's money had cost her. "Yeah," said Tracy, "but that'd be like asking Michael. And neither of you guys... neither of you... I'm not your—"

Ashley punched the girl in the arm to shut her up. Punched her for real this time. Then she went back to smoking.

"Ow," said Tracy.

"I got one of those waiting for my dumb cousin, too."

"What'd Mom do?" asked Tracy.

"You ever hear that it takes a village?"

"What does?" Tracy asked Ash as she inhaled.

After a beat, Ashley blew a column of smoke from her mouth that would've made Smaug proud. "Raising a child," she said, and she sounded annoyed that nobody understood that.

THAT NIGHT at Michael and Jenna's table, Michael explained to Ashley that he had a task for her. Jenna blushed and ducked her head as he went on—she even whispered something to him about whether or not he really wanted to say this while Tracy was still at the table—but he didn't stop, and probably *couldn't* have, even if he wanted to. He was a man on a mission.

"What I want, my dear sister, is for you to take my wife out and get her laid."

This, he explained, was the only way he'd ever stop feeling guilty for all of the shit he'd almost done with other women over the years. All the times he'd been tempted. And that one time when he might've succumbed but was too drunk to know for sure.

"So it's still all about you," Ashley told him, and now it was Michael who blushed.

He mumbled something. When Ash asked him to speak up, he said that he was pretty sure Jenna wanted this as well.

"Do you?" Ashley asked Jenna.

"I mean," she said, not able to look Michael as she spoke, "who doesn't *want* to? Who doesn't at least think about it?"

"You have your eyes on anyone in particular?" Ashley asked her.

Michael laughed. "Thomas Edward Patrick Brady," he said.

Ash grimaced. "Even after the Super Bowl?" she asked.

"That wasn't his fault!" said Jenna, and they all laughed awkwardly when they remembered that it kinda *was* his fault. If they were being honest.

"Okay," said Ashley. "But seeing as he doesn't live anywhere near here, *and* he's banging a supermodel these days—"

"But she's pregnant," said Michael, nodding like he'd just made an excellent point. "Maybe he's looking for a little something on the side."

Ashley and Jenna turned on Michael at the same moment and gave him a rare synchronized eye roll.

"No," Jenna finally admitted. "There's no one in particular."

But Michael swore that there would be, if only Tracy and Ashley would take her out. If only she'd give it some time.

And so, the three women got themselves dolled up while

Michael called the cab he hoped would make him a cuckold. He tried to offer his perspective on Jenna's ensemble as the girls made their way out the door, asking if she might not want to go for something more revealing, but the ladies gave him a triple eye roll and that shut him up right quick.

In the cab, the first thing Jenna told the other two was that she wasn't fucking anyone. She wasn't that into the idea after all, but she *did* want to shut him up about it.

"My husband," she sighed, "the guiltiest of the guiltless."

"He's persistent, though." That's what Ashley told her. And Tracy nodded along when Ash said it.

"What are you going to tell him?" asked Tracy.

"I don't know," said Jenna, and she sighed again. "Maybe I'll make someone up."

"Or," Ashley told her, "you could, you know, find someone real and maybe just suck him off a bit." Then she threw up her hands as if to say *why not?*

After a moment of silence to consider Ashley's proposition, the three of them roared with laughter. Ash and Jenna were both still doubled over when Tracy caught the cabbie checking them out in his rear view. He didn't seem all that impressed, so she gave herself a once over. She adjusted her bra a bit. Her Spanx, too.

Then, as she tucked everything back into place, she had a thought. "Shit," she said. "I just realized. You guys could get into way more places if I wasn't with you."

Ashley gave Tracy a gentle shove. "We need to get you laid, too." That's what she told her stressed-out niece. "18+ is fine by me," she said. "Jenna?"

"Oh," she said, nodding. "Absolutely. I am *so* ready to MILF it up."

AND SHE *SO* WAS. Jenna said she wasn't going to fuck anyone that night, but Tracy thought she might as well have. The way those boys stumbled off the dance floor after just one song grinding on her, the way she let their faces get *this* close to her neck on the slow ones—this close, but no closer—it was like watching a master at work.

There was this one guy, his hands on Jenna's hips like he was holding on for dear life, and she let him hook his fingers under the hem of her skirt. She had her arms up over her head, crossed at the elbows, and her eyes were closed like she was lost in the music. And maybe the dude saw this, and took the fact that she was holding her body so close to his as a kind of permission, an opportunity to make whatever move he wanted to make, because the next thing Tracy saw was Jenna's skirt riding up a bit. And then a bit more. And soon she was seeing the bottom of Jenna's ass and wondering if her aunt had gone commando for the night. And wondering how far she was going to let this go. But then, just at the last second, Jenna's arms slid down from the sky. Her fingers slipped between the slick locks of the guy's deconstructed coiffure. And then her hands were on his neck, and she was pulling his lips to her cheek. His cheek to her lips. Her lips to his ear. Then, finally, she whispered something to him and he nodded, so slight a movement that Tracy wouldn't have caught it if she weren't staring so hard. Then he backed off, as Jenna smoothed her skirt back down, back the way it was.

When Jenna turned to face him, the kid had his head hung low. Like a puppy waiting to have its nose pushed into the puddle he'd just made on the kitchen floor. But she didn't shame him, not at all. No. Instead, she lifted his chin. She lifted his chin and she shook her head to tell him "Nuh-uh. None of that." Then Jenna pointed a finger at Ashley.

The guy nodded, Jenna wagged a come-hither finger toward her sister-in-law, and Ash sauntered out to greet them. Once they were properly introduced, Ash moved in to finish the kid off, and

Tracy laughed. It was like the end of a tag-team wrestling match, only her aunts didn't high-five when they switched places.

They saved the high-five for later, once that kid was sitting sweaty with his friends and trying to wipe the shit-eating grin off his face.

Tracy was at the bar this whole time, stirring the ice at the bottom of a glass and trying to decide if it was time for another Diet Coke or time to finally break the seal. She was stirring still when the best-dressed kid in the place sidled up to her and asked how she knew Ashley and Jenna.

"My aunts," said Tracy.

"Hot," he said.

"Not sisters," she said.

"Still hot," he said. And he nodded at the two older women with a look that seemed more envious than lustful. "Their moves are too good for straight people," he said.

"Hey," said Tracy. "I'm straight. And I can dance."

"Sweetie," he said, and he touched her shoulder with just the slightest brush of his finger tips. "That's not what I meant."

"Oh," said Tracy. "You meant that the breeders aren't worthy of their prowess."

At the sound of the word 'breeders,' he tilted his head at Trace and raised an eyebrow. He wondered if he'd misjudged her, if she was truly as straight as she claimed to be.

"Straight," she said. "I swear," she said, and she held up the three fingers of the Girl Scout salute. "Much to the chagrin of my best friends back home. And my moms."

"Moms?" he said. "Plural?"

Tracy nodded.

"And those," he said, pointing out at the dance floor again, at Ashley riding Jenna's leg like it was a mechanical bull, "those are your aunts?"

"Yep," said Tracy. "It's a fun family."

And Tracy must've gotten caught up in watching Ash and

Jenna after that, or watching the crowd watching them, because the kid beside her had to touch her shoulder again just to get her attention.

"Yeah?" said Tracy, turning to face him. He was biting on the end of a finger, his feigned nervousness a kind of flirtation.

"Do you have any uncles?" he asked, raising a hopeful eyebrow.

※

"DID YOU HAVE FUN?" Ashley asked Tracy late that night, as they waited for a cab with their heels in their hands.

Tracy did a pirouette right there on the pavement and giggled as she stumbled at the end of it, drunk on relief and too many sodas.

"What if I stayed the whole summer?" asked Ashley.

And it was now that a sleepy Jenna chimed in. "How is that even a question?" she asked, without opening her eyes, without schlepping her ass off the cold concrete. "You're staying."

※

THEY MADE A GAME OF IT, hopping from island to island—from one adventure to another.

After a moment of reflection at the Arizona Memorial in Pearl Harbor, they drove up north to the Polynesian Cultural Center in Laie to take in the pageantry of the boat parade. After the luau that night, Tracy and Ashley spent the ride home debating who was hotter when they were shirtless and spinning sticks of fire: the Tongans or the Tahitians, the Samoans or the Fijians. All along the drive down the Windward Coast, and all along the H3—from the tunnel burrowed beneath the remains of ancient Koʻolau to the transcendent beauty of the Halawa Valley —the ladies did their best to make Michael cringe with their girl talk. And when that didn't work, they asked him which of the cultures was *his* favorite. Which kind of dude would he dare not kick out of bed?

"Personally," he said, "I think the whole conversation is a little culturally insensitive." But when his sister punched him in the arm to get an answer out of him, he finally admitted to Ashley that he liked the Māori best of all.

Each time they came back to Oʻahu, Ashley and Tracy hooked up with Michael and Jenna. But each time they hopped to one of the other islands, they went on their own.

On Maui, they watched the sun rise from atop Haleakalā. Then they biked down the slopes of that dormant volcano as the light of a new day washed over them. They rode past pineapple fields on their way to the Pacific, then jumped in the water for a pre-breakfast swim. And they flirted with everyone along the way, from the bike guides who gave them their safety briefing to the old couple who sold them their coffees in Pāʻia—trying to get a smile out of everyone they came into contact with.

One smile *at least*, sometimes two.

It was on Kauaʻi that they spent most of their time, and it didn't take long for Tracy to realize why. This was where Ashley and Robin had spent so many meaningful days together, away from the rest of the world. And so, everything on the "garden island" was a mixture of bitter and sweet. From the Tree Tunnel in Kōloa to the rusty orange rubble of the Russian Fort, from a kayak trip on the Wailua to the Spouting Horn at Poʻipū Beach— there was a tear for every smile, and a smile for every tear.

It was only after they'd each taken a swing over the same river where Indiana Jones had once swung—on the same rope, or so the guide leading the off-road movie tour told them—it was only then that Ashley said something about what she was feeling.

"I need closure," she said, as they hiked up to the remains of the gate from *Jurassic Park* for one final photo op.

"How do you want to get it?" Tracy asked.

CLOSURE. That was how they found themselves out on the precipice of Waimea Canyon that afternoon, Tracy leaning against an enormous wooden sign while Ashley traced the indents of the yellow letters with her finger. Thirty-four hundred feet up, Tracy marveled at the valleys of green which broke up the vast sea of pink and brown rock. But with the wind being what it was that day, she couldn't keep her thoughts to herself forever.

"You're not worried about pulling a *Lebowski*?" she asked her aunt.

Ashley ceased her tracing of the letters with the final 's' in 'Division of State Parks,' then gave Tracy a smile. As she rose from her crouch, she even gave a little laugh. "There's not much left," she said, nodding toward the backpack they'd brought with them—and the bag of ashes within—"and besides, we're not half as dumb as Walter."

And yet, Tracy still worried about getting a fistful of Robin's remains blown into her face and looking like the punchline of a Coen Brothers movie.

"A pinch for every place I ever played," said Ashley. "That's what she told me. And this was the last place," she continued, "aside from our apartment, that is."

"She brought her guitar out here?" asked Tracy.

Ashley nodded as she pulled the bag of ashes from the backpack. "She brought her guitar *everywhere*. Just in case."

Tracy gave her aunt's arm a sympathetic squeeze. It seemed like the thing to do, until it didn't. Then she let go.

Ashley unzipped the bag and made a few tentative steps toward the cliff. "I don't know what I'm waiting for," she said.

"Closure," said Tracy, offering a kind smile.

Ashley tried to smile back, but she couldn't. She knew something Tracy didn't know—something she couldn't tell the girl even if she wanted to, because it would sound too crazy. There couldn't be closure, not yet. There was a still a kiss waiting for Ashley and Robin. The voice in her head, her future self, had promised that much. And maybe that was why Ashley was holding back. Maybe she didn't want to let go, because letting go was the last thing that stood between her and that last kiss—however and whenever that promised pleasure was meant to happen.

Maybe she didn't want closure, after all.

"I've been meaning to ask you," said Tracy. "When I gave you the potion a couple years back, did you ever find her?"

Ashley shook her head. "I tried," she said, "but no."

A pained look flashed over Tracy's face, a look she rid herself of almost as quickly as it came—but not so fast that Ashley didn't notice. The kid wanted to say something, but wasn't sure if she should—maybe even wasn't sure if she *could*. It was up to Ashley whether or not to press the issue.

She didn't. She pretended like she hadn't seen a thing, and she returned her attention to the task at hand.

"I feel like I should say something profound," she told Tracy, as she held the bag out over the edge. "But I never did that at any of the other places—"

"So why start now?" Tracy added, finishing the thought for her.

Ashley nodded. Then, taking a second to make sure the wind was blowing *away* from them, she scattered the last earthly remains of her late great love into that most gorgeous of gorges—the place the brochures called the Grand Canyon of the Pacific—and she waited for a whiff of "closure," as if it was something that might blow by gently on the breeze.

۞

A FEW DAYS LATER, their glorious summer together was over. Over too soon, as all good times are and must be. After a drive across the Big Island to read messages spelled out in white rocks along the moon-like side of the road, and after a helicopter ride above Volcanoes National Park to see lava forming new land right before their eyes, they were at the airport in Kailua-Kona and getting ready to say goodbye. Ashley was bound for the mainland, and Tracy was bound for O'ahu and the next school year.

As they stood there awkwardly, girding themselves for the emotions of the hug to come, Tracy thumbed through her email and found a note from financial aid. It said she was all set for the next year. All set for the rest of her degree, too. Tracy gasped, held a hand to her mouth in disbelief, then asked Ashley if she knew anything about that.

"Surgo ut prosim," said Ashley, and she nodded her head at Tracy in a little bow.

Trace knew the phrase all too well. It was the motto of good ol' Kimball College back home, where Silvers like them had been going for over two-hundred years—way back when it was a girls' finishing school.

"I rise that I may serve," said Ashley, as if she was worried Tracy had forgotten the translation. As if she didn't know Tracy better than anyone, as if she'd forgotten that Tracy never forgot anything.

Tracy knew that Ashley had tried college a couple times, but that it had never stuck and she had no student loans to speak of.

She knew that Ashley didn't pay any rent to her parents for the use of the second floor of their house back home, that they wouldn't take money from her even when she offered—not even that time she got her father drunk and shoved six Benjamins into his pocket after he'd passed out in his recliner. Ashley had found the six hundred in an envelope under her door at the top of the stairs the next morning, with a note from her mother which read "Nice try."

Ashley had made a lot of money in her life, and she had spent very little of it. That was her reality.

She had only two vices: cigarettes and comic books. But even there she lived frugally. *Too* frugally for someone who worked as hard as she did. She rationed her cigs to a certain number per day and no more. And she allowed herself only a certain number of monthly pulls at the comic shop. If she wanted to start reading something new, something old had to go.

Back home, everyone wondered—when they looked at the yoga pants and t-shirts she lived in day in and day out—where all Ashley's money was going. But Ash knew. She had a plan.

Ashley *always* had a plan. Tracy just never expected that Ash had a plan for *her*.

"But how am I going to repay you?" said Tracy, struggling to hold back the sobs she hadn't expected to let loose until the hug goodbye.

Ashley smiled and repeated herself: "Surgo ut prosim."

And maybe she saw then that Tracy was going to fall over under the force of her generosity—that her niece was going to collapse beneath the gentle weight of Ashley's one expectation: that she give as freely as Ash when her time came—because it was then that Ashley opened her arms wide and drew Tracy into them.

Tracy cried and cried, but Ashley didn't. Or, if she did, it was a real trick, because Tracy listened to her auntie's heart through the ear she'd pressed to the woman's chest, listened to Ashley breathe mindfully in and out, and not once did the rhythm of her body change. Not once, until Tracy spoke her last words that day:

"I was born to one mom," she said. "She gave me another by marrying Desiree, and I thought I was blessed then. But now," said Tracy, through tears and snot, "now I realize there was a *third* mom out there for me, too."

"What?" said Ashley, and her heart skipped a beat. And Tracy was never sure if Ash asked her to repeat herself because she couldn't understand her the first time, or if she just wanted to hear Tracy say it again.

Tracy pulled away from Ashley just enough for Ash to see her eyes, because she didn't have the breath in herself to say it again.

And Ashley must've seen what Tracy was saying, seen it right there in the way that the girl looked at her, because *that's* when Ashley broke.

Tracy would never know that it was also because Ashley could hear in her head what Tracy thought in the next moment.

Mom was the mother of my childhood, thought Tracy. *Desiree the mother of my growing up, and you—you will be the mother of my growing old.*

Tracy never said that out loud, because she thought it sounded too corny, but it didn't matter. Ashley, thanks to those powers of hers, heard it just the same. And she didn't think it was corny at all.

It took them a long time to let go of each other completely. When they did, Ashley wiped at the corners of her eyes with her index fingers and flicked the tears away from herself. Then, with one hand set back upon Tracy's shoulder, she scanned the terminal for something. Trace turned to see what Ash was looking for, then she spotted him. Over by the arrivals gate, a man stood with a half-dozen fresh leis draped over his outstretched arm.

The loud speaker announced Ashley's final boarding call, but she said "They'll wait." She looked at Tracy and said she wanted to the girl "laid" one last time before she left. Then she took hold of Tracy's hand and rushed them over to the guy with the flowers. He said something about the leis being meant for arrivals, but Ashley gave him her sad puppy eyes and he told her to go ahead.

She grabbed one and draped it around Tracy's neck. But as she went back for a second, for one for herself, the guy flinched. This stopped Ashley dead in her tracks, and she pouted as she asked him "Haven't you ever wanted to lei two girls at once?"

He rolled his eyes at her pun, but he smiled despite himself. Then he nodded at his arm for Ashley to take what she wanted.

From the window of the terminal, Tracy watched Ashley race across the tarmac. The backs of her flip-flops slapped between her heels and the pavement. It must've sounded like applause,

Tracy realized, at least kinda-sorta, but she kept waiting for the universe to turn on her aunt. She kept waiting for Ashley to miss a step and break a damn leg. But she didn't. She made it to the staircase leading up to her plane and she slowed as she made her way past an exasperated attendant.

At the top of the stairs, just before she boarded, Ashley turned and squinted to find Tracy in the distance, to find her beyond the glare on the window. Once she did, she smiled and shook a hang-loose sign at her niece. Then she did something that was pure Ashley: she lowered her hand below her waist and shook the sign at Tracy again.

Inside the terminal, Tracy couldn't stop laughing. On her first day at college, her orientation leader had spent a fair bit of time explaining local customs. The freshmen had all seen the hang-loose gesture before, and he knew that, so to keep them from drifting off the orientation leader said, "Just remember, ladies: never throw that sign below the waist." Then he smiled a knowing smile. "Unless, you know, you want a lot of attention."

Ashley disappeared into the dark bowels of the plane as the setting sun painted the sky, as the sky painted the clouds, as the clouds turned a picture that had been one thing one moment into whatever it was going to be in the next.

Tracy didn't know what was next. Not yet. In later years, she'd wish that she *had* known. Because as hard as she stared at the tiny windows of the plane that evening, trying to find Ashley before she was gone, she would've stared even harder if she'd known what was coming.

She would've stared forever.

She might have been staring still.

❧ 13 ❧

Back in the day, Ashley had slept with half of her brother's four-piece. And seeing as she had no interest in fucking her brother, that meant there was only one band member left to cross off her list. But when she booty-called Billy one night to pitch him the idea, she was surprised to learn he didn't pitch a tent in his pants at the suggestion.

Billy and David were a thing now, in case she hadn't heard. And though that blew her mind, Ashley kept her cool and decided it wouldn't be *so* bad if she gave David another shot too. So she told Billy she was up for the package deal.

When he asked what she meant—he'd always been a bit dim, that one—she repeated the word "package" in the sexiest voice she could muster, trying hard not laugh while she said it.

"Oh," said Billy. "*Package*," he said, and then chuckled. "I get it."

And that was how Billy and David became Billy, David, and Ashley. And when she learned that Billy was out of work now thanks to the great recession, and David was still working on his dissertation, she invited them to move into the apartment she kept upstairs at her parents house.

❧

STIRRING beneath her covers one morning, months later, Ashley asked her mother if she was washing their dishes again.

Mum was. She was washing the dishes of Ashley's trio at the sink that had been Mum and Dad's once upon a time, back when they were the young couple and Dad's parents were the ones living downstairs. The sink was Ashley's now, but Mum would never forget when Ash was small enough that she gave her baths in it.

Ashley's brain buzzed at the sound of the thoughts Mum was having. Her head ached, but then her heart ached too. Because Mum was being hard on herself again, as was her wont.

I was hopeless as a mother—that's what Mum was thinking as she washed the dishes, that and how hopeless it made her feel. She'd trained to be a pediatrician, for Christ's sake, but she couldn't even care for her own kids.

Mum remembered how she ran around the apartment with Ashley on her hip, Michael at her heels, and a textbook in her free hand—always trying to do too much, always forgetting what had to be done.

She ended up changing Ashley's diaper on the goddamn kitchen table more often than not. And she was terrible at it. She had the worst timing. One time, as Ashley's pee began to puddle on the placemat, Mum got so flustered that she picked the girl up, whirled her around, and held her over the sink to finish the job.

It was filled with a half-dozen coffee cups now, that sink—brown cream congealing at the bottom of each. In the spaces between those mugs sat salad bowls lousy with dressing and flecks of kale. And on top of it all? Mum had to laugh. On top of it all was an ash tray Ashley had sculpted in art class once upon a time, in the last years that an ash tray was an acceptable project for elementary school. *She made it for Father's Day, right?* Mum wondered. And it must've been around the time of *The Goonies*, because Ash had etched a crude skull into the bottom, a skull and crossed swords instead of crossbones.

The ash tray was Ashley's now, too.

"Ma?" said Ashley, sitting up in bed.

Mum took a look at her daughter then, as she set another dish into Ashley's filthy strainer (which she realized, only at that moment, she should've washed first). Mum looked at Ashley and she wondered—Ash's hair a tangle of sweaty snarls atop her head, streaks of mascara dried and caked on each of her cheeks—how she'd gotten to be such a mess.

And it wasn't just Ashley's face. It was this whole place, this space that had been their young family's living room in some bygone age. The mattress was on the floor. A flatscreen TV was propped precariously on top of a Playstation on one side and an Xbox on the other. And on top of the milk crate that doubled as a nightstand and a bookcase stood a lava lamp whose contents hadn't moved since Ashley had bought it at a Spencer's when she was in high school.

Or was it a Hot Topic? Mum wondered. Did they sell lava lamps back then? They sold figurines to edgy tweens now. Edgy *tweens*. Mum wondered if Ashley had been that old when she was still so young?

"Ma?" said Ashley again.

Mum sighed and told Ashley there were flies.

"There's *a* fly," she said. "His name's Jeff."

Mum groaned. There it was: this tone Ashley had been striking since she was a kid, this *attitude*—a posture even, once she'd learned to stand up—and it always meant that they were in for a row. The only buttons Ash loved to push more than Mum's were the buttons on her joysticks. And even that had become a close call in the years after Mum decided Ash was old enough for her to push the girl's buttons right back.

"The fly's name is Jeff?" said Mum, feigning stupidity, even though she had a pretty good idea where Ash was headed with this.

"Should I have gone with Goldblum?" she asked.

Mum sighed again, exasperated for effect. "What you *should* do," she said, "is get dressed."

Ashley stood then and shuffled toward her dresser in a pair of fuzzy socks Mum had bought for her some ten years before. Fuzzy, yes, but ratty now too. Mum shook her head. In a masterful *sotto voce* that betrayed the theater degree she'd wanted but never finished, Ashley said, "Must go faster, must go faster."

"You've got an hour," Mum reminded her.

And now it was Ashley who sighed. "It was a joke," she said, rolling her eyes at Mum. "It's what Jeff Goldblum says when—"

"—when he and Will Smith are trying to get away from the aliens," said Mum, sure that she'd gotten it right.

"No," said Ashley, breathing deep through flared nostrils to keep her cool. "No. That's what he says when the tyrannosaurus is trying to eat him from out the back of a jeep."

Christ, thought Mum. If this was going to be one of *those* fights, she was going to change the subject. She wasn't in the mood, and couldn't understand how Ashley could be either. Didn't the girl know where they were going that day? Didn't she understand? Mum turned off the sink's faucet and asked her daughter if she still wanted a ride to her appointment.

"Do *you* still want to drive me?" asked Ashley.

Mum said that she had to go into the office anyway. Ashley told Mum that she was pretty sure it was her day off. Mum sighed and said there was a set of twins to be seen, that they had the croup and their mom was a helicopter parent.

To which Ashley replied: "And you're the only co-pilot she trusts?"

"God is her co-pilot," said Mum. "If her bumper sticker's to be believed."

Ashley didn't laugh, but she did stop talking for a second. And she smirked as she shook her head. There was that, at least: the smirk and the moment of silence. Each of those had to be worth a point. If she was doing the math correctly, Mum swore she was gaining on her daughter.

"I need a smoke after that," is what Ashley said on her way back to the bed.

Mum asked if Ashley thought that was a good idea, given the circumstances.

"Ma," said Ashley. "I didn't find the lump on my lungs."

Mum said that wasn't funny, but inside she decided it was. She would've laughed. She would have, if only Ashley wasn't her daughter.

"It's my last one," said Ashley, in a tone that almost sounded like she was asking for permission. *Almost.* Only she hadn't asked Mum's permission for anything since she'd learned to forge her signature in the sixth grade. "Last. Butt. Ever," she said.

"Where have I heard that one before?" asked Mum, before she had the sense to imagine what Ashley's retort might be.

"Oh, I don't know," she said. "Where *have* you heard that one before?"

Mum hadn't had a cigarette in eight years. Fourteen, if they didn't count the one she'd bummed off Ashley the day Dad and his chainsaw fell out of the tree outside the kitchen window.

"You see," said Ashley, plopping her ass back on the bed and giving Mum the kind of shit-eating grin only a child can give a parent. "Progress. Is. Possible."

But then, as she went to tap her last butt out of the pack, then —*finally*—the joke was on her.

What came out of the pack that morning was not a cigarette. No. What came out of the pack that morning was an avalanche of green M&M's. They spilled onto Ashley's comforter, tumbled down into the folds of her sheets, and rolled down the gentle slope of the mattress to slip between her legs.

Ash asked Mum if *she'd* done it. She hadn't, but Mum smirked and asked "Did I?"

"Ma!" she shouted.

"Maybe it was Billy," said Mum.

"He's not that clever," said Ashley as she searched her bed and nightstand for her phone. "Besides," said Ashley, "Billy's back in the spare room. I'm with David right now."

"I thought you were *with* both of them," said Mum. "And that they were *with* each other."

Ashley leapt to her feet with a groan, the M&M's tumbling onto the floor too—as if they were chasing her, as if they were *taunting* her. Her stomach grumbled as she stormed into the kitchen.

Ash opened the fridge and found it empty. The last of the English muffins were gone. The milk, too. So she went to the cupboard. But all that was left on the otherwise barren shelves was an unlabeled can of something. Soup maybe, but she couldn't be sure. The paper had been stripped from it, except for the pieces that clung to a single strip of glue which ran from top to bottom.

"Sometimes," said Ashley, collecting her phone from the kitchen table.

"Sometimes what?" said Mum, having forgotten what they were talking about.

Ashley dialed someone on her phone. "Sometimes I'm with both of them," she clarified. "But the two of them bicker about blurred lines and..."

Mum laughed as she sat against the lip of the sink. "Who can blame them?" she asked. "When one falls out of favor, you banish him to the 'spare' room." Mum made finger quotes to emphasize her point.

Ashley held a finger to her lips to shush her mother. Then she held the phone closer to her ear.

"He sent me to voicemail," she said, a mix of annoyance and admiration in her voice.

It couldn't have been more than two rings, so Mum suggested that maybe he was in a meeting.

"His outgoing message is interminable," said Ashley, her foot tapping against the linoleum of the floor. Though, with the fuzzy socks on, she barely made a sound.

"Surely code monkeys have meetings," said Mum, using the term David used to describe himself and his new job.

"Oh, sure," said Ashley. "Over Fritos, Tab, and Mountain Dew."

"Is that another ref——?" Mum began, but Ashley shushed her again.

Then Ash held the phone to her ass. And at the beep, she let fly the fiercest fart Mum had *ever* heard. Which was saying something, considering the thirty-plus years she'd been married to Dad.

Satisfied, Ash hung up and tossed the phone back onto the kitchen table. It bounced toward the edge. Once, then twice. Mum thought it was going to fall, but Ashley didn't seem to care.

It was only then that the smell reached Mum, the stench of sulfur and eggs. She pinched her nose to keep from gagging, then asked Ashley what she'd eaten the night before. But Ashley's eyes lit up at the sight of something behind Mum and she stepped right past her mother to grab whatever it was from atop the refrigerator.

A second later, Ashley plonked a Santa Claus cookie jar onto the kitchen table. Then she beheaded it and shoved her arm down the jolly old elf's neck. Mum winced as Ashley's nails scraped the ceramic bottom.

"Shit," she said.

"I've got cookies downstairs," said Mum. "If you have a craving."

"That's not what we keep in there," she said. Ashley crossed back to the fridge and yanked open the freezer.

"Pot?" Mum asked. "Your father's got some downstairs for when the boys come down to jam. It's in the—"

Ashley slapped the freezer door shut and asked Mum if there was a mason jar in the sink, if she'd washed one. When Mum said there wasn't, Ash cursed David and fell to her knees to search through the mountains of dirty laundry that formed the unofficial border between kitchen and bedroom.

Once Mum saw that Ash had begun to search through David's jeans, she asked if Ashley needed some money. Until recently, Ashley been supporting the guys entirely on her income from the club. And though she swore she was fine, that she didn't need any help, Mum wasn't so sure.

"I'm not leeching off you," said Ashley. "Not anymore than I already do."

"Consider it a loan," said Mum. "I'll go get—"

But Ash cut Mum off then. She cut her off as she yanked a receipt from one of David's pockets. "Do you know what this is?" asked Ashley, shaking it in Mum's general direction.

"What's it for?" Mum asked.

"The Splash Page," said Ashley, naming the comic book store that had been the haunt of Ashley and her friends since time immemorial. "So," she said, "he can have his vices, but I can't have mine."

Mum said that she remembered when comics were Ashley's vice, too. But the girl didn't respond to that. Instead, she tore apart her bed's covers until she found her purse.

Ashley already knew what she'd find, knew from her trip to the packie the night before that she was down to the last dime of the weekly allowance she'd set for herself. But she looked anyway, dumping the coin into her palm. Then she ran a thumb along good old FDR's profile and stuffed him into her pocket.

"That's it," she said. Ashley stood and raged out of the room, stomping the not-quite-stomps of a woman in fuzzy socks.

From the other room, Mum heard Billy yelp in fright and call out "What's the big idea?" He stumbled into the room where Mum still stood, clad only in his boxers, his laptop clutched to his chest and resting upon the ledge of his ample gut. A pair of headphones hung limply from the side of the computer as he asked Mum "What's up, Doc?"

She sighed and gave him a smile. "Nothing much," she said, "you wascally wabbit."

"Wabbit?" he said, and Mum rolled her eyes as she shook her head.

"It's exhausting," she told him, "trying to remember which of you I'm supposed to talk to like I'm on an episode of *Gilmore Girls*, and which I'm not."

"Well," he said, taking a seat on the window sill, "I'm the dumb one, Doc."

"How could I forget?" she asked.

"I don't know," he said, closing his laptop. "I *am* the drummer."

Mum told him that she'd heard the second drummer drowned, trying to make a reference he *would* get—their band had played that song once, hadn't they?—but no. All he did is look confused and ask if that made him the third.

"I thought I was the only drummer," he added.

Mercifully, Ashley's phone chimed at that very moment and he called out to her. "Ash!" he shouted. "Your phone."

Ashley returned to the room with a cardboard box stuffed with comic books. She plopped it down on the bed, squeezed between Mum and Billy, and grabbed her phone off the table.

"What an asshole" is what Ash said as she thumbed her way through the text.

Billy asked her what the message said, but Ashley didn't say. She handed him the phone instead, so he could read it himself.

Then she dropped to her knees again and began to rifle through the box of comics.

"I'll bring the groceries," Billy said, reading aloud from the phone's screen. "The M&M's should tide you over until then." Billy looked puzzled. "But what about me?" he asked.

"There's a can of something in the cupboard," Mum told him, waving absentmindedly in that direction.

"Yeah," said Ashley, plucking one bagged-and-boarded comic book from the box. "This one," she said, handing it to Billy. "How much will you give me for this one?"

The cover was mostly orange, with close-ups of four heroes set in the middle of circular crosshairs. These were set off to the right to reveal the scowling visage of a silver-haired tough guy with a glowing eye, a spiked bracelet, and an enormous handgun. The cover price? A buck in 1990. The value now? At least a carton of cigarettes, Mum imagined, maybe more.

Billy examined it as Ashley got dressed, then looked up at her with a raised eyebrow. He said: "This is David's."

"He owes me," she said, pushing her feet into a pair of still-laced sneakers, pushing them in so hard Mum worried she'd break a toe. Or two.

"Ash," said Billy, shaking his head, "I don't know."

"Enough for a carton of smokes?" she asked, pressing.

Mum said "I thought you were quitting."

Billy said that Ashley had been saying that for weeks now. She leered at him for that confession, then he broke. "I could give you more if it was graded," he said. "Of course, you know that."

Ashley told him that she'd forgotten more about comics than he'd ever know. And he nodded, so Mum guessed this was true.

"Wallet's on top of my dresser," he said. "Take what you need."

As Ashley dashed out, Mum reminded her about her appointment.

"I'm just running to Quik-Mart," said Ashley. "I'll be right back."

THE ELIXIR OF DENIAL

"Ashley," said Mum. "Your hair, your face—you're not even wearing a bra."

"Good point," she said. "I might not even need the cash."

And then she was down the hall and into the spare room. Mum asked Billy what he saw in her daughter, but Ash was back before he could answer.

"Trying to be a gentleman?" asked Ashley.

He stuttered, but couldn't get anything intelligible past his lips.

Ash mussed his hair and told him "It ain't worth the effort." Then she was gone.

৩৯৩

MUM FOUND an overturned laundry basket amongst the refuse and began to move the mountains into it. As she tidied, Mum told Billy that she'd never understand why Ashley made this room her bedroom. He and David were sleeping in a perfectly habitable bedroom with room to spare. Whatever the arrangement between the three of them, Ashley could've slept in there too. Couldn't she?

"But that was her brother's bedroom," said Billy, stooping to help Mum with the dirty clothes. "Back in the day, I mean. That room was Michael's. So maybe she'd feel weird—"

"She can sleep with each of her brother's bandmates in turn, but she can't do it in his old room. Is that what you're saying?"

"I guess," said Billy, and he scratched at the bald spot on his head, as if he might uncover the answer under some patch of dandruff clinging to his numb skull.

Together, they stripped the sheets from the bed. Then he said, "You asked me what I see in her. Real question is: what's she see in me?"

Mum squeezed his shoulder, sorry that she'd touched a nerve.

Downstairs, a door slammed open and then shut. Ash was

back, and she was stomping up the stairs. Once she was through the door, a carton of cigarettes tucked under her arm, Ashley went straight back to the box of comics. Then she started to pull books from the box.

"Whatcha doing?" asked Mum.

"What are *you* doing?" she asked, pointing at the ball of bedsheets Mum hadn't realized she was still holding. "Huh, Ma? What are *you* doing?"

Mum stuttered.

"Too much," she said. "As always."

Billy pointed at the comics Ashley had tossed haphazardly onto the floor. "What are you doing with those?" he asked.

"Making room," she said. And then she stuffed the carton of cigarettes into the box, into the gap she'd created. She shoved the lid carelessly back onto the top of the box, then carried it back towards the spare room.

"What are you doing?" asked Mum.

"Repaying the favor" was all that Mum heard as Ash made her way out.

There was a loud bang. And then Ashley was back.

"Billy," she said, grabbing a brush from god-knows-where and pulling it through her tangled hair so hard that Mum worried she might have none left by the end of her assault on her scalp. "You better clear the shit off David's side of your bed. He's in there with you tonight."

Mum asked Ashley if she knew what she was doing.

"He played a joke on me," said Ash. "I'm playing one on him."

Ashley gathered up the discarded comics from the floor and dumped them unceremoniously into the garbage can.

"Sacrilege!" said Billy, affronted. He held a hand to his chest as if he might swoon at the sight of his girlfriend's disrespect.

"Oh," said Ashley, stepping into the kitchenette. "I can do better."

She grabbed a can opener from a drawer and the lonely tin can from their cabinet. Then she made her way back to the trash and began to crank open the can.

"Ashley," said Mum, as Billy took her arm to steady himself.

The top popped off the can, which turned out to be a can of SpaghettiOs, and fell onto the top-most comic in the trash. It slid down the length of the plastic poly bag the comic was kept in, leaving a trail of red-orange sludge in its wake.

Billy fell to his knees like a child in prayer, like a desperate man in mourning.

"Ashley," said Mum, holding up two hands and imploring her to stop. "Your appointment."

Ashley glared at Billy, then at her mother. Then she slammed the can down on the kitchen table and stormed out of the room.

Mum listened to her stomp down the stairs as Billy fished the comics from the trash, brushing spaghetti sauce off of each poly-bagged treasure with his bare hands. And it was then that something occurred to Mum.

"She didn't take a pack," she said.

"What?" he said.

Ashley hadn't opened the carton. She hadn't taken a pack. Maybe, just maybe, she *had* listened.

Maybe, thought Mum, *finally*, she was winning.

"Ma!" Ashley shouted from downstairs. "Let's go."

14

Mum felt her eyelids burning—*swelling*—as Ashley delivered the punchline to the group. "Talk about chestnuts roasting," she said, and everyone but Mum roared with laughter.

What did Mum do instead? She ducked out of the living room without excusing herself. She didn't really need to, after all. The fact that she'd even been in the room, socializing instead of washing the china—that was strange, notable. That she was gone now, that was just par for the course.

In the kitchen, her hands busy in the sink, she tried not to think of the joke at all. But when she couldn't escape it, Mum did what she had done so often in her life: she subjected the troubling thought to scrutiny. What was it about the joke that she couldn't bear? What was it that drove her over the edge? That it was about an ex-boyfriend, one Ashley had rejected for the audacity of trying to love her? Well, in the years since Robin's death, dumping partners for being too decent had become *de rigueur*—just as commonplace for Ash as hiding from conflict in the kitchen had become for Mum. So, no.

What it came down to, really, was that Ashley was joking at

all. Mum set the gravy boat in the strainer to dry and moved onto the turkey platter, nodding as she went. That was it, she decided. Her daughter, as per usual, didn't understand the gravity of her own situation.

༂༈༂

THE WAY ASHLEY told the story of her teeth and the washing machine, it was harmless—an *accident*. Her brother was in Cub Scouts at the time and their father was the Pack Leader, which meant that meetings happened at their house. One of the boys, Billy Mills, claimed to be a bigger pro wrestling fan than Ashley. The other boys—save Ashley's brother, who knew well enough to stay quiet—teased Billy, asking him what did that prove, asking him how a girl could be a bigger wrestling fan than a boy anyway. Ashley paused her video game—Super Mario in early tellings of the story and Duck Hunt later, because she liked the idea of the laser gun as a prop—and she challenged Billy to try a wrestling hold on her, promising she'd get out of any move he chose.

Billy looked stumped as Ashley stalked up to him, this girl in sweatpants and a Bart Simpson t-shirt. He stuttered as he backpedaled out of the living room, through the dining room, and into the kitchen. The cartoon on his antagonist's t-shirt was telling him not to have a cow, man. But he was about to. He sure as heck was about to.

"Name your hold," said Ashley, "The Million Dollar Dream? The Cobra Clutch? The Figure Four?"

"Full nelson," stammered Billy.

The boys gathered round, some of them in the kitchen and some in the cramped hallway that led to the dining room and beyond. Where was Ashley's father during all of this? Probably smoking a butt outside. And what about her brother? He stayed silent, as was his wont.

Ashley turned her back on Billy and held her arms loose at her sides. "Let's see what you got," she told him. "If you've got anything at all."

Billy passed his arms underneath Ashley's, grasped his hands together behind her neck, then yanked her arms backward and upward. He cranked his hands forward on her neck, and she gasped. But it wasn't long before she turned the gasp into a laugh.

"That the best you can do," she said, "*Animal?*"

"Animal?" said Billy, confused.

"George Steele," she said, scoffing, starting to wiggle her way out of the hold already. "George—The *Animal*—Steele. The full nelson is his *thing*, jerk."

Billy, embarrassed, tightened the hold. Some of the boys laughed, but some were murmuring about letting her go. "She's just a girl"—that's what they said. But what Ashley heard was "She's *just* a girl." That 'just' was emphatic in her ears.

She checked her surroundings and maneuvered Billy toward the washing machine. The plan, in her mind, was to swing her whole body forward and down, so that Billy's big stupid head bounced off the heavy lid.

But for once in her life, things didn't go according to Ashley Silver's master plan. She misjudged the distances and how tightly Billy was holding on. So, when she threw her body forward, it was *her* face that hit the old maroon monstrosity. There was a loud *thwack* and Ashley collapsed to the ground, crying as much in disgust with herself as in pain. She spit a triangle of front tooth out onto the floor as Billy backed away.

"What the hell?" said Billy. "What the *frickin* hell?"

"You win some and you lose some," murmured Ashley. Then she punched Billy in the nuts for good measure.

***

IT WAS ALWAYS Mum who took the kids to the doctor. A doctor herself, she knew how to communicate with "those people"—or at least that was her husband's excuse for laying it all on her shoulders. When Billy knocked out that piece of Ashley's two front teeth when they were kids, it was Mum who took the day off and brought the Ashley to the dentist for the reconstruction. She was the one whose hand Ashley squeezed as each new instrument was set into her mouth. She was the one who took her daughter out for pizza afterward to get those new chompers good and dirty straight away.

Years later—*this* year—Mum had been the one to take Ashley to the oncologist.

When the doctor gave his recommendation—when it was Mum who was in tears and not Ashley—Ashley took her mother's hand, squeezed, and said, "They're just tits, Ma."

Mum looked at Ashley, dumbfounded. Then she looked to the doctor to see if he was still there, to make sure this wasn't some dream she was having after having passed out.

"They've always been more trouble than they're worth," said Ashley, cupping her breasts, giving them each a jiggle.

Mum slapped her daughter then, waiting just long enough to see Ashley grab her cheek in pain before she walked out of the office—waiting just long enough to be sure her daughter was still human.

Nothing rattled Ashley. That was the thing about her, the best thing. But this, this diagnosis and the picture that had just been painted for them—that should have shaken her to her core.

As she stepped outside, Mum reached into her purse— plumbing its depths for the pack of cigarettes that hadn't been in there in years. When she realized what she was doing, she began to cry again. *A cigarette?* she thought. *Now?*

Behind her, the door to the doctor's office slammed open. Ashley stormed out.

"Ma," said Ashley then. "What the fuck was that?"

"Mum," said Ashley now, in the kitchen. "Where'd you go?"

Even with the table between them, Mum leaned against the

door to the outdoors—as if she might need to make a run for it any second. She looked up and sighed.

"Would you like some help?" asked Ashley.

Mum looked over the mess of dishes and utensils strewn across the table, plus the pile in the sink and what she'd already set into the strainer. The conversation was going to come eventually, Mum realized, so why not now? She nodded Ashley toward the sink. "I'll wash, you dry," she said.

They passed ten minutes in silence, passing dishes between themselves, careful not to touch each other on the handoffs. This wasn't the first time they'd fought—not by a long shot—and they'd become old pros at dancing around each other's demons at this point. They'd been at each other's throats for more than thirty years now, from the days when baby Ashley loosed her bladder on the changing table with regularity—with *flourish* even, and with giggles—through her years of couch-surfing between her friends houses to avoid coming home after a fight, to this latest debacle. Thirty-plus years. At the thought of the number, Mum cried again.

"Jesus, Ma," said Ashley, turning off the water and pulling Mum into her arms.

Mum rest her head against her daughter's chest and wept. The sound of Ashley's heartbeat was loud and fierce in Mum's ear. It was steady, as sturdy and reliable a muscle as it had ever been. And just as naïve. It had no idea, did it—that strong, pumping thing—it had no idea what horror lurked just atop it. Mum listened for the sound of the beast that would kill her daughter, but it was silent; it wasn't the sort of villain that went in for bombast or any of that. This cancer was there to do its job and nothing more. It wasn't seeking glory, only the end result.

"Ma," said Ashley, "I'm going to be okay."

"Don't tell me that," said Mum, pushing away. "Don't you *dare* tell me that."

"Mum," said Ashley.

"I am a *doctor*," said Mum, tapping one fist against the girl's chest, and then another. "Don't you dare try and tell me you'll be okay. You have *no* idea, and you have no business making promises that you can't—"

Ashley took hold of Mum's fists in her hands. Then she spoke. "I didn't make any promises," she said. "I didn't say I was going to live forever. I just said I was going to be okay."

They looked at each other for a moment, mother and daughter, before they broke into uneasy smiles.

"I'm going to be okay," Ashley said one more time.

⚜

SOMETIME LATER, when the house was finally empty and it was just the two of them in the living room with the Hallmark Channel on the TV, Mum asked Ashley what the joke was, the one about the chestnuts roasting. "I wasn't really listening," she said.

Ashley's smile broadened. "We were camping, and the dumb shit sprayed bug spray on his jeans—'We used to do this in Scouts,' he said, 'on a dare'—but when he jumped over *our* fire..." Ashley trailed off, starting to laugh already, even before she'd finished the joke. "When he jumped over our fire that night, it *actually* happened."

"*What* happened?" asked Mum.

"For the first time in his life, that little liar's pants really *were* on fire. And so," Ashley began, and she rolled her open hands, one over the other in her mother's direction, hoping that Mum would catch on and finish the sentence.

It took a second, but Mum *did* get it. Then she chuckled. A little at first, and then a lot. And then a lot more. "Chestnuts," she said, in between snorts of laughter. "Chestnuts roasting on an open fire!"

"Except," said Ashley, "the only thing on him as big as a

chestnut was something he probably hoped was a lot bigger." She held up a pinky finger and and waved a little hello with it.

"Or longer," said Mum, "at the very least."

And now they were *really* laughing. Laughing together, falling into one another. Laughing and crying, crying and laughing, so loud and with such gusto that they weren't sure where one feeling ended and another began.

15

S he'd worn a sun dress through the thunder storm, and she'd paired it with a goofy grin that betrayed the kid she'd always be inside. But even when the dress was soaked through and she was shivering and the people on the trolley could see everything there was to see of her, Ashley didn't care. She didn't care because she wanted them to see, wanted them to gawk.

"Where are her boobs?" a small boy asked his mother.

"Never you mind," said the mother, turning his face away.

"They're gone," Ashley told the boy, who was peeking at her through his mother's fingers now.

The mother stood, took the boy's hand in her own, and walked him to the other end of the train.

Ashley grabbed hold of one of the overhead handrails to steady herself. Then the train lurched out of the station at Lechmere, toward the Science Center and the river beyond.

"You get yourself a new phone?" asked an older fellow, pointing at the white bag she held, the silver apple on its face.

"I did," she said.

"Those things'll give you cancer," he said.

"Well, I've already had that," she said. She pushed the dripping bangs of her wig away from her wet forehead. "Doesn't that make me immune?"

He chuckled. "Wouldn't that be grand?" he said.

"Just like the chicken pox," she said.

He nodded. "Everyone should go through it once."

"Makes a man out of you," she said, with a fierce nod of her own.

He chuckled again. "Not much left in the world that'll do that," he said. "Not in these days."

"Oh," she said. "I don't know. Maybe all it takes to make a man is the man himself."

He smiled. "And perhaps," he said, "someone to tell him that."

☙❧

WHEN THEY WERE THROUGH, she was worried about him. She'd heard heavy breathing before—even prided herself on inducing it—but this was something else.

"You okay?" she asked him.

"Wasn't sure I could still do that," he said, panting.

She wanted to ask him when the last time he'd done it was, but she was afraid of how he might answer. So, instead, she brought it back to her and asked him if he'd ever been with someone this flat before.

He said nothing for a moment, as if unsure how to answer—as if uncertain their banter on the train could continue here. With her naked. *Exposed.* Then his face lit up with a wide smile.

"Yes," he said, slapping his knee. "Took me a minute to remember her name, but as a matter of fact I did. Hannah was her name. Sweet young thing when I came home from the war on account of my Purple Heart. She'd've been the last one picked at the whorehouse, if you take my meaning, but those boys didn't know what they were missing. She was a great kisser, that

Hannah. Mmm hmm. And pretty as all get-out, long as you kept your eyes up where they belonged anyway."

"Like a gentleman," said Ashley, smiling as she tried to keep the thought at bay. This couldn't be him, could it? The soldier from way back when, the soldier from the days to come. Could it be? His flat-chested girl was called Hannah? *Hannah*, of all things? The name Ashley had been using on stage since she was 18?

"A gentleman," he said, as if trying the word on for size for the time in his life. Or the first time in a long time, at least. "A gentleman," he said, and he looked little sad—he looked as if he might have come to the conclusion that he wasn't worthy to be called one. But then he nodded and said "I suppose so."

✦

WHEN THE CANCER CAME BACK, it hit her first. But it hit Sean the hardest. *Sean*—that was his name. They'd spent three days in bed together before she'd worked up the courage to ask for it. Then she remembered that she'd never gotten the soldier's name back in the day. And so, the name Sean didn't mean anything anyway.

"Can't hardly take a piss," said Sean. "It's into my balls," he said, massaging his wrinkled sack, hairless now because of the treatments.

"Mine, too," she said, replacing his hand with her own, cradling him, not sure whether something more vigorous would hurt or help.

"You have balls now, have you?"

"Ovaries," she said. "Same difference. They were the same, in fact, back before we were babies."

He set his hands on her abdomen. "Whereabouts are those things, anyway?" he said.

She pulled his hands lower, until they were in place, until the inside of her ached at his touch.

There was a tear on his cheek. "You'd think He could have spared one of us," he said.

He. Ashley couldn't bear the thought of that capital H, the one she was sure she'd heard in his reverent tone.

"Maybe he did," she said. "He spared *me* the disappointment of believing in him."

He looked as if he were about to say something, his tongue slipping past his teeth, his chapped lips. But then he pulled it back, held it in.

"I hope you weren't expecting a prayer from me," she said, "once you're gone."

He laughed. "A prayer?" he said. "Hell no. I'm Irish, Ashley. All I expect is for you to get plastered and cry in your Bushmills."

❧

SHE DIDN'T GO to the wake. She'd never been properly introduced, after all, and she didn't feel like explaining herself to the niece from Manhattan who was running the thing—that woman who was older than she was.

Instead she rode the subway, sipping whiskey from a paper bag and trying not to stare at the bald kid who got on at Charles-MGH—the hospital stop—a pale boy with headphones like hers. A phone like hers, too. She tried not to tell the joke, the one Sean had told her the day they met. But when the kid smiled at her, she couldn't resist.

He couldn't resist either. When she asked him to come home with her, he looked into her eyes and he said "Yes" without a moment's hesitation—without a moment to look down and see what he was in for, what he was missing.

❧ IV ❧
TEARIN' UP MY HEART

2013

16

In the end, Ashley's mantra became "Today is not the day." She said this to anyone who asked how she was doing, or how she was feeling. And she said it to herself, over and over, on the days when the pain was so bad she couldn't even get out of bed.

"Today is not the day," she said. Even on the last day, the day she died, this was what Ashley told the women who sat at her bedside.

Two weeks before, when the folks at the hospice asked her where she wanted to spend her final hours, she said "Sandwiched between Vin Diesel and Dwayne Johnson." And when no one said anything in reply, she added quickly that she wouldn't be mad if they brought Elsa Pataky along with them. But when pressed for a serious answer, she'd told them "at the house down the Cape." And that's how she'd ended up in the living room of her grandfather's old cottage, surrounded by not only her mother—who'd barely left her side for the past six months—but also by Veronica, Desiree, and Tracy.

Every day she could manage it, Ashley hugged Vern and Des long and tight for letting her take over their living room—which was the only downstairs room big enough for the hospital bed, and had the best view of the ocean besides. And every day, whether she could manage it or not, Ash hugged Tracy.

The girl had just finished her sophomore year at U of H, and Ashley asked every day for more details. She couldn't be happier to see the change in the kid's demeanor, the dramatic change a simple financial contribution from Ashley had made to Tracy's peace of mind—and her grades, too. But it wasn't the academics that Ash wanted to hear about the most. No. She wanted to hear about Tracy's new boyfriend instead, the Hawaiian hunk whose pictures filled the girl's phone these days. And though all Tracy's moms seemed to care about was whether the relationship was serious or not, what Ashley was more concerned about was how *seriously* the dude had rocked Tracy's world.

"Details," she demanded. "I'm living vicariously through you now. Details," she said again. "It's my dying wish."

"And speaking of last wishes," said Ashley's mum.

Ashley groaned, said "Ma!" and tried to leave it at that. But Mum wouldn't leave anything alone these days. It seemed her only way of coping with Ashley's impending doom was to get practical. Practical, and practically emotionless.

"Will you finally write a will?" Mum asked. "Or tell us whether you've decided about cremation vs. burial?" And what about this? And what about *that*? Mum had a million questions, one for every tear she was holding back, and all Ashley had for her in exchange was the mantra.

"Today is not the day."

Because how could it be?! Ashley stared out the living room window, stared longingly at the ocean, and thought about everything that was just beyond her reach. She thought about all that she had left to do—all that she just plain *knew* she had left to do. She still had to kiss Robin one last time. She still had to find her way back to 1944, to Sean, to the place where she'd *seen*—with her own two fucking eyes—that she had more life to live.

"Ashley," said Mum, taking hold of Ash's forearm and giving it a gentle squeeze. "Today *could* be the day. You don't know."

Ashley sat up and proclaimed she was going to the beach.

Mum and Vern and Des protested, ever the responsible adults now, but Tracy said nothing. Instead, she moved to help Ashley out of bed, to give her support as they searched the house for something Ash might wear.

⚜

THAT NIGHT, more tan but also in more pain, Ashley slept fitfully. She was so restless, in fact, that, for the first time since she was a little kid, she asked her mother to tell her a bedtime story.

Mum looked up from the book she was reading, a trashy romance with a busty wench on the cover, and asked Ashley to repeat herself.

"A story," said Ashley. "I can't sleep."

Mum dogeared the page she was on, then set her paperback aside—atop the cardboard sleeve of photographs she'd been rifling through absentmindedly for the past few days (whenever she wasn't reading or watching her soaps or pestering Ashley, that is). "What did you have in mind?" Mum asked, removing her glasses and setting them atop the book.

Ashley was glad her mother hadn't chosen to simply read aloud, but she didn't know what she wanted. That was the problem. If she'd known that, she could've told herself a story in her own head and gotten herself to sleep.

Fortunately, Mum could tell. She had a knack for knowing what Ashley was thinking. And so, she started in on something and Ash closed her eyes to listen.

"Here's one I've never told you," said Mum, "the story of a camera and its long journey home.

"A long time ago, with no help from his father, your Grampy had to bury his sister. To pay for it, he sold most of the things she owned. It wasn't much, because she was a poor artist who'd spent the last year convalescing in a sanatorium, but it helped. And sentimental as he was, he couldn't bear to look at all those cameras and canvases and easels of hers anyway.

"Well, of course, you know that years later your brother became rather enamored with his late, great aunt's work—"

"Obsessed," said Ashley, smiling at her interjection.

"And so," Mum continued, "Michael began to hunt down anything of hers he could find. And he asked me to help. That's part of how I came to spend so much time at garage sales and flea markets over the years. According to your grandfather, his sister had marked everything she owned with her initials. So anytime I saw an old-timey camera on a table of junk for sale, I couldn't resist checking the thing for the letters D.S.

"And then one day, a week ago, on that day Vern and Des told me to take a shower and get out of the house for a couple of hours, I found one: one of Great Aunt Dottie's cameras. So of course I bought it. And get this, Ash: there was a roll of undeveloped film inside."

Ashley opened her eyes for the first time since her mother had started the story. She looked at Mum and raised an eyebrow. Then she asked "Did you get them developed? Is that what those are?" asked Ashley, nodding at the sleeve of photos under Mum's book.

Mum nodded and reached for the sleeve. "And here's the craziest thing. That camera's been around. And whoever had it last, they took a picture of *you*."

"Ma!" Ashley shouted, as she took the photos from her mother, "how in the hell was this story going to *ever* put me to sleep?"

Mum blushed and gave a nervous chuckle. "I wasn't thinking," she said. "You asked for a story, and this was the first thing that came to mind."

Ashley flipped through the photos, looking for the one in question—flipping past nudes that Great Aunt Dottie had meant to paint someday, snapshots of 50s-era cars that Gramp might've taken himself if he'd kept the camera, and a half-dozen of some 60s kids growing up in front of a white picket fence, before ending up on a portrait which might've been plucked straight from her own memory.

The photo was of Ashley and Young Sean, because of course it was. He was in his uniform, looking sharp as a knife, and Ashley was dolled up like a Vargas painting—curves to spare, even with two of her best curves gone. The two of them were cozied up together behind the window of a familiar-looking bar—The Strumpet's Sister, of course—and they looked so, so happy.

Ashley teared up at the sight—a fact not lost on Mum, who squeezed her hand. In the photo, Ash was leaning into Sean, supported by the arm he had around her back. And she was planting a big, wet kiss on his cheek.

"I notice it's not the first kiss you've given him," said Mum, pointing at the lipstick smudges along Sean's neck—including one *just* peeking out from beneath the unbuttoned collar of his shirt.

When Mum asked "Who is he?" Ashley didn't answer. She couldn't, because Mum would never believe her. What was she supposed to say? That this was a photo from the future, even if it looked like a photo from the past? Ashley's head hurt just thinking about it—and she wanted that to stop, because she hurt enough everywhere else already. So she focused her attention back on the photo, on the way she would bend her leg when this moment finally happened—one leg bent at the knee and kicked back into the air behind her, a heeled shoe dangling from her toes.

See, Ashley said to herself. *Today* can't *be the day. I still have this left to do.*

"I didn't mean to get you all riled up," said Mum, taking the photos back from Ashley's shaking hands and slipping them back into their sleeve.

Ashley felt her heart all aflutter, but then felt the cancer stab at her from all over in protest. "No," it seemed to say. "I'm going to kill you." It seemed offended by the very idea of life coming back to her, at the stubbornness of that organ at her core which refused to give up.

"Ash?" said Mum, and she squeezed Ashley's hand again.

Ashley squeezed back. "I'm okay, Ma," she said gently. "It's totally weird, that photo, but I'm glad you showed it to me. Gives me something to dream about," she said.

Mum nodded as she let go of Ashley. Then she stood to tuck her daughter in. "Was he someone special?" asked Mum. "I don't remember ever meeting him," she said.

"No," said Ashley, giving a weak smile. "I don't think you ever did. Sorry."

Mum bent to kiss Ashley on the forehead. When she stood up straight again, there were tears in her eyes. It was the first time Ash had seen her mother cry in months.

"What?" she said.

"There's so much of you I'll never know," said Mum, running her fingers through the short, matted locks of hair Ashley had regrown since stopping chemo.

"There's always tomorrow," said Ashley, closing her eyes.

"Right," said Mum, out there somewhere in the darkness. "Tomorrow."

But tomorrow didn't come for Ashley Silver. Death came instead.

17

The next thing she knew, Ashley was haunting her own funeral. And it was the strangest sensation of an existence that had been full of odd feelings and experimentation. Aside from being dead when she was sure she shouldn't be, at least not yet, there was the fact that she had no body to speak of—not even some ghostly shade of the woman she'd once been. No. There was no Ashley in the room. No *one* Ashley, that is. Instead, there seemed to be two dozen of her in the funeral home that morning—an Ashley for every person who sat there crying over her corpse. Indeed, she seemed to exist only in the space between the breaths that each of them took—memory after memory after memory calling her back from whatever came next.

It was excruciating. She would've begged them to let her go, if only she had a voice with which to make a sound.

The least worst part was when someone was speaking, for the crowd of them seemed to focus then on just one memory instead of several. And so, it was during the speeches that Ashley was able to be most present—whatever "present" meant in these in-between days.

Her brother spoke first, overdoing it as always, trying to make a pulpit of the funeral home's simple, secular lectern and stand. But for once, Ashley truly appreciated Michael's predilection for the preposterous. His vision of himself as an orator of old, as a public speaker *par excellence*, kept all the attention on him. And that gave Ashley all the energy she needed to keep herself collected.

"I try to imagine," Michael began, speaking aloud to the spirit his atheist ass claimed he didn't believe in, "I try to imagine what was going through your head on that last day, as you lay on the beach trying for one last tan.

"And what I imagine is you with your eyes closed, trying to focus on the rancid smell of the empty clam shells strewn all around you—that undeniable scent of our childhoods down the Cape. You're trying to focus on that rank odor, that pungent stench, until the pain in your abdomen is gone, until all that there is in the whole wide world is the midday sun on your skin and the funk of the dunes in your nose.

"In the house behind you, Veronica is fussing—making calls, tapping out text messages—letting me and the rest of our far-flung family know that it's almost time. You're trying to drown that out, too. Not that you feel guilty, just annoyed. I can see your brow furrowing at the very notion of people wasting time on your expiring husk. There is still life out there for them to live. Why aren't they out there living it?"

Michael paused here to look out at the crowd, and for a moment their feelings of guilt—and the memories of Ashley attached to those feelings—began again to tear her apart. But then, mercifully for once, Michael yammered on.

"The pain won't go away," he continued, "so you give into it, thinking of it finally as an equal. You imagine it devouring your insides like you used to devour sleeves of Oreos when we were kids. The pain is every bit as voracious as you once were, its hunger nigh insatiable.

"But you don't focus on it for long. You can't focus on

anything for long right now. When a breeze ripples the triangles of fabric covering your flattened chest, you think of the breasts the cancer took from you. Then, as goose flesh rises across your midriff, you think of the ovaries missing deep beneath your cooling skin. And you dream for a moment of the children you said you were going to have when you were a little girl, when the moms gathered at a party wouldn't leave you alone until you gave them an answer—an answer that was a lie, I should note, because even then you knew you weren't ever going to have kids. 'A boy and two girls,' you told them. A boy and two girls who you imagine now. You told the moms that you'd let your husband name the kids, whoever he might be. Even though you already knew you didn't want a husband. You already knew you didn't want anyone or anything to weigh you down once you were ready to go."

Michael paused again—whether for effect or because he honestly needed to stop himself from crying, Ashley couldn't be sure. "You were always so good," said Michael, "so good at telling people exactly what they wanted to hear.

"If that's what *you* wanted them to hear, that is. Sometimes— and with me it was more often than not—you told us what we *needed* to hear instead."

Michael sniffled back something there, some emotion, and Ashley almost wanted to give the poor sap a hug. Almost. Then he took off his glasses and rubbed at them for a moment with the absurd tie he was wearing, the one emblazoned with the gathered superheroes of the Marvel Universe—a gift she'd given him ages and ages ago, after a panicked Christmas Eve shopping trip to Newbury Comics.

She wanted to smack him upside the head for being so senti- mental, so maudlin.

With glasses back on his face, he continued. "Suddenly," he said, "you feel a shadow passing over you, a weight on the side of the beach chair you're laying out on. You open your eyes and find

Tracy sitting there, squeezing sunscreen from a brown bottle into her open palm.

"You tell her that you're not really worried about UV rays at this point.

"'Yeah,' she says, 'but do you want to leave a burnt corpse or a tanned one?'

"I like the thought of Tracy being there," said Michael, "a kindred spirit with a hand to squeeze when the shudders come. I like the idea of you not being alone. And I'm happy knowing that Tracy knew what to say when you began to cry from the pain, when the last great veneer of your guarded, watchful life began to tumble down. I'm comforted by the fact that she knew that what you needed most in those final moments was a joke.

"It makes me sad, though, that Tracy still hasn't told me what it was, what punchline pulled the last laugh from the worn-out and worn-down body of Ashley Silver.

"'It's private' is all she'll tell me. 'Girl stuff.'

"So, I'm left to wonder, left to wonder what I would have said to you if I'd been the one there on that beach with you in those final moments. What would I have said when you told me to fuck off that last time, with a twinkle in your eye that you hoped would betray the love behind your jab? Would I have stopped applying the lotion, the lotion I'd had to pop a Xanax just to get up the gumption to lather onto you? Would I have stopped, toweled off the excess, and stalked away like I always did when confronted with that audacious strength of yours, that strength I'd never had myself? Or would I have found the courage to finally love you the way you needed to be loved? Would I have had the strength at long last to match your stare and stay silent until you rolled onto your stomach, wincing as you did, and told me:

"'Don't forget my back, asshole.'

"I don't know," he said, pausing dramatically—but not without a heaping, helping of sadness to make the drama authentic for once. "I'll *never* know."

TRACY'S EULOGY CAME NEXT, the meat and potatoes of the festivities—a recap of Ashley's life that felt a little paint-by-numbers to Ashley, but who could blame the kid? She'd never lost anyone before, let alone someone so dear to her.

At the end though, she let down her guard a bit and decided to share with the gathered masses just how grown-up she'd become in the last couple of years—to show them that Li'l Tracy wasn't so little anymore.

"The joke I told her," said Tracy, "the one Michael mentioned, is the kind of thing you can only tell to certain people—to people who understand that, to paraphrase Emily Saliers of the Indigo Girls, sometimes we *have* to laugh, because we'd cry our eyes out if we didn't."

Tracy paused and took the measure of the room, and Ashley wished in that moment she could whisper in the girl's ear to "fuck their feelings" and tell the joke no matter what. But she couldn't, so she just had to wait.

"So," said Tracy, "since I'm thinking at least half of you can get behind that sentiment, and since I think it's *exactly* what Ashley would want me to do, I'll tell you the joke I refused to tell Michael until now."

Michael smiled up at her, a silent plea to "go on." Ashley would've smiled too, if she had a face to smile with.

"Knock, knock," said Tracy, gesturing with her hands for the crowd to respond.

"Who's there?" they replied, the whole chorus of them.

"Nine-eleven," said Tracy, growing red as a beet.

"Nine-eleven who?" came the automatic response, before any of them had a second to realize what punchline they might be setting up.

Tracy frowned, gave them a face approximating that of a sad

puppy, then spoke the punchline in a faux-whimper. "You said you'd never forget."

Half the room roared with laughter. The other half shifted nervously in their seats. And as Tracy took a seat between her two mothers—both of whom were laughing—Ashley thought there could've been no better tribute to her memory. She felt for the kid, who'd put herself out there in front of her family for the first time and defied them to be indifferent. Ashley wanted to tell her "It gets easier," that "it gets more fun." But of course she couldn't. All she could do was hope that the hugs of Tracy's mothers, a sandwich of love around the tearful girl, would communicate what Ashley could not.

Across the room, another hug sandwich elicited quite a different response in the still incorporeal Ashley. Her brother was being smothered with support from both his wife and from Mum. And though Ashley could stomach her sister-in-law treating her poor husband like a broken thing her love could fix, the sight of Mum treating Michael like he was a child and not a thirty-six-year-old grown-ass adult—that was too much.

Ashley knew what Mum would say if she could see Ashley now, if there was any of Ashley left to be seen. "Why do you hate your brother so much?" Mum would ask.

And what would Ashley say in return? "Christmas," she would say. "Christmas 1995."

When she'd stepped into the bathroom that evening, there was a cigarette floating in the toilet.

She didn't flush it right away, much as the sight of it made her gag. No, she stared at it for a moment instead—ignoring the pleas of her bladder to get on with it. She stared and she sniffed. And then, having smelled nothing while standing up straight, she bent at the waist to take a deep whiff from a closer distance. But still: nothing.

Atop the lid of the toilet's tank, Ashley set down the things she'd brought with her—the electric razor she'd stolen from

Michael's Christmas haul, and the bottle of hydrogen peroxide she'd lifted from the shelves of Page's Drug the day before. Then she peeked behind the green and red curtain Mum had hung over the linen closet for the holidays. And that's where she found the tall canister of air freshener Mum had used to cover her tracks.

Or to try and cover them, Ashley thought, looking back into the toilet bowl and frowning at her mother's failure.

It had been more than a year since Ashley had seen her mother smoke, since Mum had *promised* at Grampy's funeral to stop. And maybe she had. Maybe Mum *had* stopped for a while. But Ashley didn't have to rack her brain to figure out why Mum had started again.

She looked at Michael's razor, thought about her ingrate brother and his expensive college, and she gritted her teeth. He didn't give two shits about what his selfish ambitions meant for Mum and Dad, how his desires might crush theirs. Half an hour away, in his cozy dorm room, he didn't have to watch Mum picking up extra shifts at the hospital. He didn't have to watch her taking on extra patients just to make ends meet. But Ashley saw. She saw it every day.

Ashley was the one grabbing Mum the extra Coors Light she needed to put her lights out each night. Ashley was the one breaking up the fights with Dad, the one telling the two of them that it'd get better when she knew that it wouldn't. She was the one. She saw. She knew.

And so, she flushed the cigarette away, sat down to do her business, and plotted how to show her asshole brother what was what.

It came to her as she stood to flush once more, the opening shot she'd take in their latest war. It came to Ashley as she caught sight of Michael's razor on top of the toilet. At first, she'd intended to hand it back to him as unbroken as she could manage. But now? Now it was going back to him in pieces. Or as close to it as she could manage.

An hour or so later, the lifeless razor discarded in a shallow pool of brown hair and dirty water, Ashley stepped out of the bathroom with a blonde mohawk. The sides of her head were buzzed, her eyebrows were gone, and all the hair left on her head reached for the sky. It reached for the sky like the pair of middle fingers she raised to salute her brother—her dumb fucking brother, who was standing in the dining room with his mouth agape.

Would he *ever* understand what he'd done? Could he?

No. Probably not. *But sure*, Ashley thought in the here and now, *give him a hug*. Comfort him for his supposedly heartfelt bull-shit. *Comfort him* Ashley thought, *instead of me*.

I mean, she thought, *all I did was fucking die*.

Outside the funeral home, the sky cracked open and began to weep—to weep the way that Ashley could not. And Ash would've wondered if she had caused it—if that's all any thunderstorm ever was: the unwept agony of some recently departed wretch—but she was too busy trying to understand how she'd even got here in the first place. She still hadn't kissed Sean in the window of that dirty old bar, something she'd seen herself do with her own two eyes. And she still hadn't kissed Robin, the love of her fucking life, a kiss she'd been promised by a voice in her head that had never been wrong yet.

"Be patient," spoke the voice, the voice which had been silent for so long. "The answers are almost here. But there's one thing you have left to hear."

The director of the funeral home was asking now if anyone else wanted to speak before they concluded the service. And it was much to Ashley's surprise that her father's hand went up. Once upon a time he'd been impossible to shut up, but Dad had grown remarkably quiet over the years since Ashley's diagnosis. Saving his voice for work, for the radio—where Doctor Al gave his classic rock listeners no hint of the pain he was enduring in the here and now—Dad rarely spoke at home these days. The only words that crossed his lips with any regularity were the words "I don't what to say."

And yet, here he was, stepping up to the podium to have the last word on his dearly departed daughter. And somehow, that sight drained all the venom out of Ashley. Outside, the rain began to fall even harder than before.

"When you were little," said Dad, "you forgot your mittens on purpose. You'd leave them tucked beneath your pillow on the days I stayed home from work to take you kids sledding at Shedd Park.

"You always asked to borrow mine when we got there," he said, "and I'd always say yes."

With a smile on your face, thought Ashley. *And a shake of your head.*

"You'd put your hands inside my gloves," Dad continued, "and make the climb to the top of the hill. And dragging behind you, attached by a length of yellow rope you clutched in your fist, was the red plastic sled you'd keep riding for years after you'd outgrown it. If it got stuck on some tree root poking through the snow, or slid off to one side on an icy patch, you'd curse it for not following your every command. But you loved that thing. You loved the thrill it made possible. And you *never* would have cast it aside, no matter how many times you threatened to.

"Last winter," said Dad, "I remember standing outside with you in the snow and telling you this story, neither of us having remembered to wear gloves. I remember the feel of your hand resting in mine, not in my glove anymore but your flesh pressed against mine. I remember what you said to me."

"You lived for twenty-four years without me," Ashley had said. "I know you can do it again."

"I smiled," said Dad, "and I nodded my head. But I couldn't stop crying, tears freezing on my cheeks, snot crusting up my damned mustache. I couldn't stop crying, because I couldn't stop thinking of myself waiting at the bottom of that hill in Shedd Park, waiting for you to make your way back to me. I couldn't stop remembering the way I beamed at you as you skidded to a halt at my feet. My brave daughter. My fearless little girl.

"I shook my head when you asked to have one more turn. I always shook my head..."

But, thought Ashley, as her father trailed off, unable to finish the story as he choked up on his tears—unable to reach whatever profound conclusion he'd been steering himself towards, and steeling himself for. *But,* she thought, *you always said "yes" anyway*.

"And now," said the voice inside of Ashley, that echo of her self to come, "we're ready."

❧ 18 ❧

When Ashley wandered back to life from whatever comes after—from whatever comes *next*—the place she wandered into was the back alley behind the Strumpet's Sister. She had just enough time to glimpse the cottonball clouds of a sky that looked eerily familiar—just enough time to wonder where the Sister was this time, and *when* it was—before her whole field of vision was obscured by a person who'd thrown themselves into her arms and was holding on like nobody's business.

After the oddity of her day at the funeral, to hold and to be held was a novel sensation—and a most welcome one. And so, even though she still didn't know who it was that was pressed against her, Ashley squeezed the person to her chest with all her might. For a few long moments, she didn't *care* who it was. She didn't care, at all.

Until she did.

As they pulled apart, it was the scent of fuzzy peach perfume which gave Ashley her first clue about who it was she'd been holding onto so tight. The second clue was the shock of bright, blue hair atop the weeping person's head. But even when the music of Robin's voice filled Ashley's ears, she still couldn't believe it.

It wasn't until they kissed, until they were kissing under the setting sun with one of Robin's hands pressed against the small of her back, that Ashley dared to hope this was real.

"See," said the voice in her head. "I wasn't lying."

No, Ashley said to herself. *You weren't*. And then, despite herself, she sighed. And she remembered that she wasn't done yet. This wasn't the order she'd hoped things would happen in, but apparently this was the way things were meant to be. It couldn't be simple. It couldn't be one last fling with Sean and *then* happily ever after with Robin. It had to be the other way around.

It just *had* to be complicated.

Robin pulled away first, and the eyebrow she raised suggested she knew that something was up. Then she said as much. "You've got something left to do," she said. "Don't you?"

Ashley nodded. "I could try *not* to," she said.

And now Robin nodded herself. "But we both know how that would go." She kicked one of the trashcans that lined the alleyway, then she asked Ashley "Where do you have to go?"

Ashley nodded at the door which led inside.

"And what do you have to do?" asked Robin, slumping against the brick wall of the place and sliding her ass to the grimy alley floor.

"Who," said Ashley. "Not what."

"Oh," said Robin, nodding as she kept her eyes on the ground.

"It's nothing," Ashley insisted. "A fling."

"Well," said Robin, nodding toward the door. "Fling yourself in there and take care of it. Then fling yourself back out here," she said, "because we've got some serious shit to take care of."

Ashley crouched down to look her lover in the eye, then took hold of Robin's chin and nudged her to cooperate. "Are you sure it can wait?" asked Ashley, once Robin was looking at her again.

"Looks like it has to," said Robin.

৩৯৯

As Ashley made her way inside, she hoped the Strumpet's Sister wouldn't be as difficult as it sometimes was. But she needn't have worried. The moment the door to the alley had closed behind her, she caught sight of herself in the mirror behind the bar. And there she was, at last: the frail beauty she'd seen with Sean all those years ago. Ashley was, as the old saying went, ready for her close-up.

And so too, it would seem, was Sean. For just at that moment, Ashley heard a wolf whistle ring out through the place. And when she searched the dim room for the person who'd made that simultaneously flattering and ghastly sound, it didn't take her long to find him. He was sitting by the front window, two sheets to the wind and working on the third.

Ashley sauntered over to him, but didn't take a seat when she got there. This didn't need to take long, and if she sat she was afraid they'd fall into their old rhythms. Old for her, that is. New for him.

"Well," he said, not quite slurring yet but on his way there. "Ain't you a sight for sore eyes?"

She smiled at him. "Long day, soldier?"

He nodded. "Wasn't meant to be," he said. "But the fella I had to visit today was a real piece of work."

"You fight in the war?" she asked him.

He nodded. "And I'd be fighting still," he said. "If not for some shrapnel."

Ashley took hold of his hand and squeezed. "You poor thing."

He squeezed back. "Just doing my duty."

"Well," she said, running a finger across his knuckles, "might I thank you for your service?"

He nodded at the nearly empty mug on his table. "Thank

you," he said, "but I've probably had enough as it is. I need to drive back to Boston tonight."

"I had something else in mind," she said, nodding toward one of the darkened hallways off to the side of the place.

"Oh," he said, and he leapt to his feet—his eagerness letting Ashley know she was right, that this wouldn't take long at all.

☙❧

WHEN THEY WERE DONE, when Sean had had his way with "Hannah" against the wall of a bathroom stall and they were on their way back to his table, the voice inside of Ashley spoke its final words to her. "We," it said, "are about to become I again."

And sure enough, just before they'd sat down, Ashley caught sight of her younger self on the street outside. And though she'd meant for years to study this moment with every ounce of attention in her, to see what had happened after she'd blacked out and how she'd ended up back on the ferryman's boat, she was blinded in that next moment by the pop of a camera's flash going off just outside the window.

Ashley wanted to curse the fool who'd taken this long awaited moment from her, but then she saw who the fool was. It was her grandfather—her grandfather as the strapping young man he'd once been—holding his sister's old camera and trying for once to do as she did, to take life as it came and to live life as the wild stallion he'd always imagined his sister to be. But when he saw the look on Ashley's face, the look of a woman he must've thought was angry for having her picture taken, the sad man dropped the thing and ran away. He ran back to the sadness he'd been fighting all day—and maybe for all of his life: the sadness about his dead sister, about his unforgiving father, and about what this world was coming to. What it was coming to moment by moment and brick by unforgiving brick.

SHE BID Sean farewell at the door—giving him one last kiss on the cheek as Hannah, then sending him off to the lifetime that stood between him and his fling with "Ashley from the train." Then she strode across the bar and made for the back door.

Outside, in the alley out back, Robin was pacing. She'd never been able to keep still, not when something was bothering her, and it made Ashley's heart full to see that some things never changed—not even after death.

"Okay," said Ashley, and Robin jumped at the sound of Ash's voice. "I'm done," said Ashley, letting loose a nervous and apologetic giggle for the fright she'd just induced.

"Good," said Robin, setting a hand atop each of Ashley's shoulders. "Because Tracy needs us."

"Tracy?" said Ashley, confused. "Why us?"

"Kid's in jail," said Robin.

"For what?" said Ashley.

"Murder," said Robin.

"Who did she kill?" said Ashley.

"Ada," said Robin, and she just left her nonsensical statement at that, waiting for Ashley to catch on.

A gust of wind rushed down the alley, headed toward the stirring waters of the river out back. It pushed the two women into each other, sending shivers down each of their spines. It was so cold and so sudden, in fact, that it shocked Ashley out of her stunned silence.

"But," she said, "Ada was dead a hundred years before Tracy was even born."

"Yeah," said Robin, and for the first time she looked honestly scared. "Yeah," she said. "I know."

The Silver Family's story concludes in The Dance of Dreams, *wherein we learn what Ada has in story for Tracy Silver and the rest of her wretched family.*

ACKNOWLEDGEMENTS

The text of Chapter 15 was first published, in slightly different form, as "What He Was Missing" in the 2015 issue of *Commonthought*.

Special thanks to Lissa Brennan, Al Russo, and Bethany Snyder for their invaluable feedback on early versions of this manuscript.

Thanks to my brother John Clark for his help with the copyediting. Any remaining errors are the result of my own stubbornness or stupidity.

ABOUT THE AUTHOR

E. Christopher Clark is the author of the Stains of Time series, a family saga with a hint of magical realism and a whole lot of time travel. His other books include the short story collections *Out of the Woods* and *Under the World*, the novella *The Seven Wives of Silver*, and a collection of poems cheekily titled *Bad Poetry Night*. His short stories have been published in *Live Free or Ride: Tales of the Concord Coach*, *River Muse: Tales of Lowell & the Merrimack Valley*, and the University of Hawaii's *Vice-Versa*. A graduate of Lesley University's MFA in Creative Writing program, he lives in Massachusetts with his wife and daughters.

echristopherclark.com

facebook.com/eccbooks

x.com/eccbooks

instagram.com/eccbooks

goodreads.com/eccbooks

pinterest.com/eccbooks

amazon.com/E.-Christopher-Clark/e/B00H0G94T0